21

DAHLIA'S IRIS AND FICTION

DAHLIA'S IRIS SECRET AUTOBIOGRAPHY AND FICTION

LESLIE SCALAPINO

Leslie Scalapino
4/16/04

FC2
NORMAL/TALLAHASSEE

OTHER FICTION BY LESLIE SCALAPINO:

THE RETURN OF PAINTING, THE PEARL, AND ORION: A TRILOGY

DEFOE

ORCHID JETSAM

Published by FC2 with support provided by Florida State University, the
Unit for Contemporary Literature of the Department of English at Illinois
State University, the Illinois Arts Council, and the Florida Arts Council of
the Florida Division of Cultural Affairs

Address all inquiries to: Fiction Collective Two, Florida State University,
c/o English Department, Tallahassee, FL 32306-1580

ISBN: Paper, 1-57366-111-2

Library of Congress Cataloging-in-Publication Data
Scalapino, Leslie.
  Dahlia's iris : secret autobiography and fiction / by Leslie
Scalapino.— 1st ed.
    p. cm.
  ISBN 1-57366-111-2
  1. Detectives—California—San Francisco—Fiction. 2. Murder victims'
families—Fiction. 3. San Francisco (Calif.)—Fiction. 4. Boys—Crimes
against—Fiction. 5. Alien labor—Fiction. 6. Widows—Fiction. I.
Title.
  PS3569.C25D34 2003
  813'.54—dc22
                            2003018474

Cover Design: Victor Mingovits
Book Design: Tara Reeser

Acknowledgments: Parts of this work have appeared in *Kiosk, Mantis, Small
Press Traffic, Enough, The Alterran Poetry Assemblage, Free Verse, Conjunctions.*

Marina Adams' collages in the chapter "Elude" are imitated as doodles
by Leslie Scalapino. Front cover photo and inside photos are by Leslie
Scalapino.

Produced and printed in the United States of America
Printed on recycled paper with soy ink

FOR TOM AND LYN AND FOR ADALAIDE MORRIS

THE PAST *IS* ONLY ONCE—YET IS A FUNCTION ONLY OF ALLUSION. SO IF THERE WERE NO SOUND OR STRUCTURING THAT'S RECURRING, THERE WOULD BE NOTHING TO FALL BACK ON. TO BRING IT TO THAT.

READING:

THE FOOTNOTES, WHICH ARE A PAST, FUTURE, PRESENT, ARE PART OF THE MAIN TEXT. MY STATEMENTS OF RELATION ARE NOT DEFINITIONS, BUT SIMPLY MOTIONS: STATEMENTS OF RELATIONS ARE MOTIONS.

LAYERS WERE ADDED TO IT; AND THE INTENTION IS TO SEE CHANGE INTRODUCED INTO THE WHOLE: NOT REPRODUCE MISTAKES WHILE BEING IN IT?

CONTENTS

NOTE ON SECRET-LIFE WRITING

This note may be read at the beginning, middle, or end of the text.

Dahlia's Iris is a novel with interior streamers streaming off of it. It is both part of my *Secret Autobiography*, which follows it, and a contemplation of the Tibetan form that is their written tradition of *Secret Autobiography*, which is not the chronological events of one's life but one's life seeing.

I think the implication of their form is: one's seeing is the instant of bringing one's faculties into question. Tibetan Buddhism's practice is a form of attention *as* the mind's constructions by seeing these.

Dahlia's Iris is divided between perceiving and actions in a space—I'm trying to bring these together on one space (throughout), where thinking and one's sensations would be (are) actions there too.

Tibetan Treasure Discovery is related to their tradition of *Secret Autobiography* (secret because it is written, not spoken to others before it's written, and is not an account of one's exterior chronological events). Earth Treasure Discovery is the finding of an object hidden in a prior life; it is found by the person who is the reincarnation of the one who hid it. Mental Treasure is one having accurate visions in one's present life.

In the movie *Invasion of the Body Snatchers*, the interior "I" or viewer being throughout consumed by the outside and the inside at once, the inside there is only a reflection of the social outside, which is alien.

The alien pod-flowers in *Invasion of the Body Snatchers* consume a self by duplicating it (its appearance): physiological is conceptual. Interiority thus destroyed by being its duplication is socially uniform: is a reflection of a U.S. 'view' that interiority itself is entity/as uniformity.

I'm viewing *Invasion of the Body Snatchers* as an inverted image of the self in the U.S. (the self as an 'original *appearance* only,' limited and fixed, which continues to appear the same by being utterly destroyed *as duplication*). The film is an inverted image of 'democracy but (as that) which has no inner practice of it.' 'No inner practice of itself' (it is not actually 'taking place,' only the image or appearance exists which has no inherent self).

As exemplified in *Invasion of the Body Snatchers*, conceptual is physical (DNA) and language. DNA is also language (code of instructions). Conceptual is structure of exterior and interiority. In reference to pod-flowers, appearance is invasion, destruction only.

Transformation as duplication is one's fiction inseparable from one's interior conversation. 'One' being entirely rendered *by* the outside (invasion)—only one's interior rendering can *be* the outside (or perceive it). One has to *be* the outside, has to articulate exactly one's interiority which *is* (and mirrors) that outside/(which is at once destroying one) in order to apprehend these.

As opposed to the tradition of anything, the *practice* of anything is interior, outside of social. In U.S. postcolonialist writings now, opposition to conceptual appropriation of other cultures is sometimes being articulated as: to confine to description of their tradition, not one's interior practice.

In the city of Babel there is no corresponding existence. Western society or one in society 'attempting to transform itself interiorly' by taking in outside conceptions—is being 'held' to a *prior conception of itself.* The U.S. is also changing the outside (world) to resemble itself.

The U.S. fits the paradigms of both *Invasion of the Body Snatchers* and *Blade Runner*, as does Tibet. The U.S. is occupied by 'itself'; Tibet quintessentially the modern state by being the inverted image: visibly contains all times, is occupied (by invaders and/or by itself), and impinged on is transforming conceptually and physically *en masse* by this cultural and material occupation.

'Written' (in my *Secret Autobiography*) is to trace 'inner life' that interiorizes the outside. While that which is 'inner' can be recognized (even by oneself) only as the inverted image of 'exterior social way of speaking and seeing here.'

I wrote this after traveling in Tibet.

My sense is that *Secret Autobiography* is (one is) to be *not* socially proscribed, isn't either 'outside' or one's 'interior,' is seeing outside *any* frame. Secret is not spoken—not *speaking* the vision at the time of writing *Secret Autobiography* (not shared and thus not socially formed before being read).

PART I: INDIGO AT NIGHT

INDIGO AT NIGHT

The visual space is authoritarian space, controlled from the air.

The collapsing vast tiered polluted ruin that is (future) San Francisco as (as if even one vast building is abandoned cities, people having moved off-world to the colonies) illuminated vertical landscape of vast tiered building-pyramid-slabs (like space platforms) are already ruins, merely the reflection of images the viewer can't see (in the 'future' retina then of the boy running, a part of the indentured labor force, without papers) of that which *he* has seen off-world before.

The off-world—the colonies are the vast unseen, of which there are no flashbacks or forward—is the enslaved present then.

One boy has been 'retired' (listed as suicide or accidental death) found apparently fallen from one of the skyscrapers on an alley. Unidentified, Hispanic, perhaps fourteen years old or twelve.

Another repetition:

The reindeer come off the ship, a herd, then another herd of them come off. The seals having been exterminated by white trappers brought famine. In black night on a desert of ice the starved Eskimo set out to hunt in the herds of transplanted reindeer now.

Detective Grace Abe wakes—opening within her lids first—having slept in her office, intercepted in sleep by Cloe (Officer Cloe O'Brien) entering speaking to her.

In Grace the thought of a day is ahead, as is a sight (though a sight is only memory instantly of something one'd seen).

You've been here all night, Cloe states. Below their police precinct tenth-story office, there's a bus stalled outside in the San Francisco street.

All the passengers are bursting threaded wet-bulb-flowers. The horn of the bus blasting endlessly. Detective Grace Abe, her lids almost closed as she's glancing downward at the bus, closes the tenth-story window.

The lips and eyes of a brown-haired fleshy woman are distorted meshed when she whines.

Seated in a café with another woman, flesh whines that she also feels grief for her friends and a loved-one who have died of AIDS but she does not have the right to feel this.

I have no right to grief (sing-song repetition is here the only language in public). The AIDS epidemic still rages, but the drug-treatment now confining the symptoms prolonging the embattled life of the ill—the number of ill still proliferate—the public is lulled, not perceiving this proliferation. It's doubling: ten years ago 40,000 new cases, now 80,000 new. The first germ-line transmissions.

The news mentions only the subject of the masses from other nations being ill. Their masses not having access to the drug-treatment is touched on in the news, so that the presence of AIDS spreading here may be hidden from the public view, Officer Andrew Chen thinks.

The regimen of trembling lips which suffocate feeling infantilize them, the public. Sentiment.

The friend, with whom the-flesh speaks, murmurs to her astonished You can feel grief, regardless of the 'right' to it. Immediately the brown-haired flesh snaps I *can not!* I *don't* have a right to feel grief.

Their conversation brushes against Officer Andrew Chen who considers it pleasantly, a moth flying on the light: on a bulb in day, the amber moth is becoming another amber moth. Andrew lifts his eyes as Grace and Cloe enter the café.

They are followed by Captain Jasper Frank, a man slumped vibrant with grey thatch of hair floating on dove's lids, lids which spill sagging on the collapsing stubbled jowls. An aging elephant, Captain Jasper Frank moves to join them at a table.

Brown-haired flesh continues her whining next to them, punctuated by the surprised friend murmuring Janice, in the background of their conversation—which is about another accidental death> possible suicide, also an unidentified, Hispanic boy found in the business district skyscrapers. He's apparently fallen, his corpse crushed by flight.

The future is seen akin to the physiological process of the amber moth.

Bifurcating, it does not progress. They flit ahead and behind, in the midst one walking appearing. One appears to be resting walking in the crowd, which flits backward at times and hanging then at the instant jets forward still as if flitting in bleached lit space that opens—they are not there. Then fills with them (people flitting into the space ahead fill it, appear even to be running).

Change is rarely seen in people walking. They don't appear to change there. One time, someone saw a man change as his character while walking quickly with the others blank, blank crowd on their way somewhere who are buoyant.

Illegal aliens are landed in small boats on the California coast at night. They are already indentured servants who are bound to work off their fare. Sometimes the traders, fearing apprehension, drowned their illegal cargo or locked them in the hold starving and thirsty. Others curled in the hold wake on the pitching sea. One has split away from the self felt in that one's skin. Before that night which is passed, a self had been felt in one person's skin.

Grace bathing lying in the bath submerged is a bead holding the soft skin under which pink pulsing capillaries hold darting. There's a cough in the hall. Someone passes. Her lids closed. And ran her hand down her side under water. Under water the side is velvet from the frame interiorly and from the hand.

1. DAHLIA

Crushing a rose. The corpse of the boy is a crushed rose on the cement in the alley below.

A boy flown at night is a kite in the black from the tenth story suite of a skyscraper wall of glass. Whirling in the sky, he lands on his back.

Dahlias are yellow in a bouquet. Detective Grace Abe submerged in it, an owl gliding in a silver day sky also submerges and is visible there (an owl somewhere else). (Don't veer, stay in one place.)

Indigo at Night is not based on realism but on repetition. It is a detective novel, a form which depends on realism only—but maybe repetition of that convention and of events will make a crack, will crack realism.

One boy has been 'retired' (listed as suicide or accidental death), found apparently fallen from one of the skyscrapers on an alley.

Another boy, two weeks before, was also found in an alley, the corpse also crushed, consistent with having fallen from a height. He'd been found several blocks from the spot of the present one, the boy who'd jumped. They're not necessarily related.

TOR dot.com is a pornography internet company, which borders the alley, the initials standing for TORRID.

Two weeks before, Officer Cloe O'Brien kneeling in the nearby alley amidst overturned garbage cans by the busted-screen of the back door of a restaurant. Hearing clattering inside in the kitchen, Cloe'd squatted on the crumpled small corpse.

About eleven or twelve years old, she estimated the corpse. Hispanic. Mostly Chinese immigrants there. He was found by a busboy who works at the restaurant, who'd been out having a smoke in the alley. Near the garbage cans, Cloe notices the remnants of a homeless person's bedding. Someone else, not the victim, Cloe thinks.

The area filled with homeless who are living in the alleys and, at night or even day, on stoops of corporate or government buildings. They have their dogs with them as Cloe strolls Van Ness, four-lane lines of cars streaming, and turns off of Van Ness into the alleys.

A gel-spike-red-hair-cut showing small mother-of-pearl ears, Cloe's mouth a soft smile speaks clearly and kindly. But no one recognizes the first boy, nor later, the other one.

Cloe had knelt there beside her corpse (of a homeless woman, once) while the priest, interviewed by the press, stated the episode would be forgotten immediately.

People will get over this in a couple of days, he'd said, as if he were dismissing sensationalism, they should get over it. Not give sensation or life attention.

So much for church, she stings inside a year ago.

Strolling now, she interviews homeless on Mission Street (the Hispanic neighborhoods of San Francisco). She asks first with one picture, then both. A boy darts away from her when she asks if he can identify the boys in the pictures. He sees the corpses in the photos and his face changes. Hey, she calls and runs after him but he disappears into a construction site.

Walking home passing by a fruit and flower stand on 16th and Valencia, Cloe forgets the day and is in only one moment in the evening. Then it's night black with lights.

The present is the same and so is different at once. In that there is war all the time.

Is everything being the same everything is different and is then romanticism one time—is that all the time? In that there is a war all the time.[1]

A man riding a bicycle as if on the open sea in that a wave traveling five hundred miles an hour is not visible in the other waves is in evening. He is barely visible. At the same time as he's swathed in evening, the hills carry him and the bicycle fast as the bicycle is in the other waves. Cars in the waves perched hanging at lights crawl or hang down on the hill.

Around 5:00 Thursday evening, Jonah Winter is dumped in California Street in front of Grace Cathedral. The corpse is naked with cuts everywhere on him. Covered in blood and curled, he resembles a cocoon.

He's been flayed quiet. His clothes were found a few yards away. The patrol cars blocking traffic which is stalled everywhere in rush hour anyway standing cars panting, Grace walks from her own car to the scene and kneels examining his cocoon. (I had a dream of someone dying then after, wet capillary case.)

She examines the clothes and wallet.

Perhaps he's aware of the very slow wave now rather than the cars that are carried invisible in it. The moon races outside the slow wave. Until he's completely outside the wave there.

Officer Andrew Chen rings the bell outside. The doorman answers. Showing their police badges, Detective Grace Abe and Andrew pass the doorman (who's calling upstairs) and take the elevator to the level of Jonah Winter's apartment.

There is Dahlia Winter, jet black hair, the mouth blurred opening Where? in Grace's sentence. Grace says, Mrs. Winter,

---

1. Gertrude Stein's view of change had to do with composition. Our composing: separation and simultaneity of action and fate. "This then was the period that brings me to the period of the beginning of 1914... Romanticism is then when everything being alike everything is naturally simply different, and romanticism... Everything alike naturally everything was simply different and this is and was romanticism and this is and was war."— Gertrude Stein ("Composition as Explanation," page 527 in *Stein Writings 1903-1932*, The Library of America, New York, 1998.)

we regret, your husband is dead, California Street Why? he's been killed.

Grace had changed. Four years earlier a meeting of occurrences had precipitated, or suddenly there was a man who had been a marine dead who was in her. She would be running out, it would be him running. But she would never leave her body or her own mind when he was there. He'd been Special Forces, an assassin when he was alive; she hadn't known him but she would feel the presence of his activities, 'ghosts of actions she had done' which were apparently his, or hers. Though she hadn't acted (when he had killed someone, before entering her).

First addicted to Ibogaine, a drug used by Indian hunters, causing illness of vomiting followed by elation and an utter lucidity in hunting, she'd spiraled with the marine being there erratically. Then addicted to a Peruvian drug derived from frogs, the secretion applied to burn marks on one's chest or arms. Cloe, Andrew, Jasper Frank were aware of her use of drugs. They were not aware of the marine who might suddenly begin and be there in her. She didn't tell them. Andrew murmured Don't Grace, finding her in her underslip burning her chest. She changed. The marine, who really was a particular unknown person, did not return.

Yet there were still flickers as if she'd known people before, whom she was now seeing. She stared at Dahlia speaking seated on the sofa in the old elegant Russian Hill apartment. Dahlia Winter rose her face splitting in a mask. Tears poured on a stretched face which appeared furious. She split apart then coldly.

She burst out but is always contained. After he'd died, one is walking across a field of high grass that is white in the sunlight and is changing to orange-rust in the wind. A trail has been cut through the grass and one hears the sound of a motor far ahead through the swaying high grass, which moves in the wind. Powdery white fog is boiling on the top of the high grass ahead, a wall of grass that sways. Dahlia Winter had repressed in being a servant pretending to be that to blame and to corrode with attack so that a man with whom she was was soon silent cringing. An image of a wrathful deity with a larvae-like figure in its mouth, Dahlia held in her mouth the bleeding cocoon, burst capillaries threading it that's him—held in her mouth, her suffering because her life was closing (his was closed)—which had never dilated to be love or to do other than close malevolence in a recurring pattern. Hearing the sound of the motor as if he's grinding by the sound in the waving field ahead. That one is or will be there to grind. Being who grinds. On the cut trail the sound enlarges as one walks and is a tractor mowing, the powdery grind of white grass flying in the fog on the white high sheets of uncut field turning orange-rust in wind.

I was always having to be a servant in pictures as a child, Dahlia Winter explains to no one. I'd wait on him too. He worked all the time like a drone, she snaps.

Grace murmurs I think you should call a friend to stay tonight, perhaps to stay a few days, Mrs. Winter. Dahlia Winter rises, in the entrance hall makes a call murmuring. They hear her return in the icy silence, her face flexing repressed.

Mrs. Winter, where did your husband work? Inventions dot.com Inc. Were you aware of him being in trouble, of there being anyone people who would kill him? No. Had his mood changed, had he appeared disturbed? He was always silent. That hadn't changed. He worked constantly. Mrs. Winter, what kind of corporation is Inventions dot.com? Dahlia Winter stares stinging Grace. Pretending she Grace had no intellect, Grace thinks. The room is lined with bookcases, filled with books. In the pause Grace feels Andrew Chen stir calmly seated beside her. Information, Dahlia Winter says suddenly losing attention and wavering. We're sorry to have to ask you these questions now, Officer Andrew Chen interjects leaning forward kindly so that Dahlia Winter's shoulders relaxing slightly shake and tears rush from her eyes.

Grace wonders is she speaking of the marriage? as if his death were nothing, or she can't comprehend his death yet.

Grace crouching in the midst of California Street on the cocoon, a curled ball of webbed bleeding capillaries—is the first instant it occurs to her to wonder if the marine had been addicted. He'd first appeared in her dead in the caustic anger of someone who was Grace's friend then.

He'd transferred into her. In the same period, Grace became addicted to Ibogaine. Events appear entwined but occur separately. Sometimes the same event appears to occur again.

She had a dim 'memory,' always in the present only, of the marine's activities but these were separate from her own actions (she did not do his actions or any resemblance of his at the time the marine was in her, or before he was in her). And these were not dreams of something she *wanted* to do either. She had no impulse to do his actions hunting killing people (though she had no specific information about his life either) regardless of her job as a police detective. He was entirely separate troubled. Running, she would find herself weeping, but as him.

Excruciating physical pain finally dazes so the person is still in their flesh. One's still, while the flesh feels as if it is existing in the outside separated. The flesh does not seem to *be* that one, yet is theirs only and enhanced delirious.

The door to Dahlia's apartment opens. The friend apparently, the one she'd called. Who lets herself in. Mrs. Winter introduces her to Andrew, Mabel Jet. Mabel Jet without words, a shocked expression there already, warmly embraces Dahlia.

They leave her with Mabel Jet.

The white field of high grass now completely mown close to, in the sense of touching, evening—where silent it's utterly white-yellow evening, the air also becomes dark, one to grind there on the mown white will occur anyway. No space of time on the completely mown white grass at evening yet grinding of the person there/people there—in visibility—will occur though it's silent white mown.

What is the relation of character to action? In "The Storyteller," for example, Walter Benjamin views fate as being character. So one's fate is not determined, is not outside oneself, because it is one's character.

But one's fate is tied to or alongside many people's characters simultaneously. This simultaneity occurs in the separation of the storyteller's speaking and the listening of those present.

Actions (physical motions) occur in between or amidst, or one's motions *are* character *as* fate at once?

One's movements in events and in time transpire separately, are not one's character—though *later* appear to be one's character. Is movement of being (physical motion even) something other than character or fate?

One's actions (motions in events) and character transpiring separately simultaneously, is the present-time repetition only?

DAHLIA'S IRIS

Dahlia's iris may have only action in it. Or the action in any present instant not visible (any sight is only a photograph of what *was* seen) may be only visible there after the action has passed (just as the light from dying stars is seen much later)—so an action isn't visible ever.

Dahlia appears to be separate, seated at lunch at Zuni's, dressed as if she is waiting for someone. She taps her fingers on the table at her place setting, a second place setting empty beside her.

Her apartment has an iris in a vase, but Cloe hasn't been there. Dahlia has not seen Cloe before.

Cloe has been following her, seats herself at a table nearby. The young officer muses Surely Dahlia has seen her (Cloe thinks, of seeing herself in third person through Dahlia's green iris). But there is no flicker in Dahlia's eyes, as if she's so abstracted that nothing passes in front of her, after her husband's death. Or did she see this blank way before? Cloe wonders, but she does not have the thought recur over and over the way Grace would.

Dōgen's sense of time and being is that present, past, and future are simultaneous; they occur at once separately and do not impede each other. A possible way of seeing this: A person who has died, is not 'dead' except when they are 'in death'—at other times, viewing their lifetime in space as also time, they are not 'in death.'

A book might be a simultaneous past, present, and future. To find out a relation that doesn't occur before, in the text.

Introduce motion and interior is in it. Only.

The order of the chapters of *Dahlia's Iris* is: to see character of people, character of an individual, at random, an invisible thin weight, prior to streams of events or a huge event—character of ordinary people, who have no impingement on those events in history—and see their weight/their relation to it. It's not a sense of seeing character as either good or bad but as if shining thin weight whose composition is grasped 'at once,' in one instant here.

To see the relation of character of people and the present instant, in every instant. That is, seeing character while (or as part of) continually staying on tracking every present instant. Even trying to track every instant changes an instant.

In the comic strip, one is separate—sight and reading are separate. Reading is unseen, is below or above and calm.

2. FLOTILLAS

Pete Debree, a partner at Inventions dot.com, is on the white field—they're seated in his office—but in the mown white or the high orange-rust flicking in the changing sky that's white shining, he's quick, alert. Yet, however keenly intelligent, affected. He has a lazy soul if there were souls, Grace apprehends—in Medieval Christian theology, a person described as committing sloth, suffering which impeding the will the person cannot rise to receive, is not receptive of, the grace of God; a form of that being the man's cynicism, corrosive laughing at one devoted— as if in that ploy of sloth he, dropping the apple of discord (or a ball in a game), doesn't have to do anything in it again in speaking to whomever stopping to pick up the apple (although it's dropped in conversation which Pete Debree seeks, enjoys), the devoted one is left (behind, having stooped to reach it) with it as a possibility or trap, anyway condition that may determine them (causal, or make them determined). He waits withdrawn watching them in their action—and not seeing the field, that one to grind in it the visible powdery white grass blown on the top of the high *waves* of grass flicking in color where one will be, he knows (meaning accepts).

So that's the mysterious thing. Accept the white field. Does he really comprehend? Yet he plays, there's this space open, stillness, though always with his background activity (that is worldly power) which he uses—mean finally, though playful and alert. She likes him. Or does she like him—it's not really expressed like that.

The expression doesn't mean anything—certainly not to him. Probably. And *this* is only an instant (of their first conversation).

He says that her way of seeing (personal, not what she's said or asked him) is insane (hers "is a state of insanity"—one being in a state of insanity embarking into or being in how she sees or the place seen/'imagined' by her). She doesn't answer that or speak. He's slipped that in (not related to the reason she's there). But she has the feeling he doesn't really think that, a ploy playful—but that he means it 'deeply,' systemic. So though one is to stoop to pick it up and gaze at it and be swept past—actually one perceives in him an alternate condition in which perception and all seeing is turned facing something else, other than one's view (seeing the two which can't exist at the same time).

The invading force, eating food killed at such an imperceptive level of cruelty (not noticed by them, the conquerors) that even their habits, their habits of *eating* disgust those conquered—who are turned anyway facing the white mown field, that it is there always. Whereas the commercial military, who'd mowed them down imprisoning and killing, are having the *intent* (the goal is) that one live a long time, have sumptuous food. Have commercial pleasure. Which to these others is impediment, is terror that is sloth of being inured (in attending wrongly, having no will to seek).

Yes, Detective Grace Abe concurs politely, but what kind of information does Inventions dot.com sell, what were the present jobs Jonah Winter was undertaking—with whom did he come in contact?

Pete Debree, enjoying her company, and presenting to her a portrait of their internet realms, swivels in his chair, lively slouched dainty hawk lighting here and there on the internet demonstrating access to distribution of mining machinery in Brazil, or in China, machinery for dam projects... So it's machinery? asks Grace. Well, yes but that's only one, we're coordinating many acquisitions and transfers of products... They're interrupted by a grey-whitened short man who enters without knocking pausing when he sees Grace with the manner of an old owl white soft creases everywhere like he's tiny rumpled or puffed feathers, she thinks.

The name is being emitted from his mouth (before he pauses), E (he refers to Pete Debree as Pete E), and his mouth and teeth seem to Grace to be the same tiny creases or white feathers as the rest of him, but with a pink opening which now hesitates irritated.

Phil, this is Detective Grace Abe. Detective Abe, this is Phil Wilson, our third partner. Pete E says, the lively dainty hawk's charm (someone who loves food and wine, but also plays a sport, tennis). She's here to investigate Jonah's terrible accident.

Aware that Pete Debree hasn't yet shown a sign of remembering that his partner died yesterday, as if the partner didn't die, Grace is now curious—Why do you say it's an accident?

Oh. He says sweetly. Well, his death. Phil Wilson intervenes Detective, what is *your* interpretation. His tone implies that when she says, as he implies she will, that Jonah Winter was murdered, her 'interpretation' of the event can only be viewed as sensationalism, extreme.

Jonah Winter was flayed, bald raw. Someone wanted something or they were amusing themselves.

The rumpled ashen creases move in intense irritation. I don't think it has to do with something here, he says.

She stands up. We're going to have to review all of your projects, files, contacts, anyone with whom Jonah Winter came in contact.

Winter's fellow partners don't seem fearful, nervous, or even concerned—either about the police or the killer (or killers) who tortured Jonah Winter. Grace states to Andrew Chen later. We're going to have to change that.

The blue of the day is unlike our paint or ink colors.

Stripped to her slip burning her chest, there's the memory of applying the secretion to the burn marks—then illness for two days (vomiting and delirium). After, a clear elation occurs, the entire day is the blue and is lucidly empty except for the figure in it for whom she's looking (the sense, almost a premonition of him before he is—in the sense that he's visible to her mind but not yet filled in by being seen).

She contemplates Andrew Chen, the memory of him having found her holding a match to her chest hurt—she'd applied the secretion anyway, in front of him—as he says softly to her, Grace Don't. It had been her compulsion to do her work.

In the thin early morning at the corner of Valencia and 16th, Cloe O'Brien walks having the memory of the man in the night when with his hands he'd cupped her head gently as he was coming between her legs. The elephant's trunk coming between her legs, she smiles softly there on the street. Stopped.

Later Grace is sitting in Captain Jasper Frank's office. She has the sensation of riding in a car through a city she's never seen, not stopping, but slowing—the illusion of the city—which she sees through the capillaries of a man.

The 'memory' occurs of a boy sniffing gasoline (to get high), he and his younger brother—'memory' of others with whom they associate, who are also parentless.

Grace Abe's eye is light and lightens the man seated quietly looking at her—as Captain Jasper Frank bends fixing two cups of coffee, swinging slowly the wilted elephant turning, the dove-lids on the lowered jowls bent to place the coffee in front of them. Grace, this is Inspector Antonio Borrero, he's from Colombia, he can shed some light on our two boys.

Antonio Borrero looks at her carefully. But she just smiles.

The lowered dove-lids concentrate on putting a cigarette in his lips, unlit, then put it aside, trying to stop.

Their memory being implants, the Replicants are romanticism. As the present, they're always in the present. In the sense that action can't be described or it's outside of itself. But it's constantly coming outside.

Andrew Chen alone in his apartment in the black night borough hacks into a vast internet of Inventions dot.com, one veiled screen leading to other constellations. His memory sticks on at present the phrase Deploy the drivers. Drivers, he wonders. It's an e-mail from Pete Debree.

Working, Andrew's mind drifts onto a weight in space. He sees his parents in horizontal space, his father's face only. His mother being eaten within lies huddled, cells eaten [Andrew's mother is dying of cancer]—he makes his mind drift to cello music, where it moves to space of: only a few cello performers are chosen to record, the same ones. In any one time, we're only hearing the same ones.

After the illness of a couple of days, Grace outside lucid runs in clear elation seeing the sun at midnight. This glimpse was available to everyone, immediately after death. They encounter [there's a sight of blank box for 'hidden'] "face to face" as the harper's song puts it. But she isn't dead. The sun and the moon come onto the same horizon (there's only one: of that instant)—where one's movement is also. One breathes yet sees the sun and the moon, separate—their motion, or not, visible—at once on a line that's horizon.

In future (or it seems to be time, of future), Dahlia's green huge iris dilated—doesn't see then—yet reflects Grace running seeing the sun at midnight.

In enigmatic writing, pictures (sights) substituted for sounds—as, jackals towing the sun barque were for the verb 'to drag.' Any bird or sight might be substituted for any other bird, so a piece of writing may be only birds (only the same sight, but with many meanings).

3. LIQUID RED OF SWALLOW'S MOUTH

The ball park of the Aztecs or Mayans, the winning team of the ball game sacrificed played in expectation of being killed for it, why do people come up with this? mutters Grace distractedly. Having to fear always, it's systemic, and people going along with it… as if they had to, or they devised it.

Andrew acerbically comments, It's entertainment and distraction from something important. Same as us.

Everything being random would be the test, that there were quiet spaces amidst the ball players unnoticed is random also.

Fear is random by being constructed everywhere. Being outside of fear is random bliss. Peaceful, it can't be controlled.

There's no meaning behind events, except that of constructed/orchestrated events—

How about random hell? queries Andrew, he's leaning back his eyes half-masked in the sun as they're seated outside at a café. He's resting. That's derived, I *just* said. Then he sips his cappuccino without opening, at his lips. Not opening either lips or eyes. Grace leaves her distraction to pause and smile slant-ways at him while his eyes almost closed there filter the soft, illumined traffic of people and dogs compressed onto a dazzling yellow bus that's before them whose huge steering wheel is slowly whirling, under the driver moving the nose of the bus around the corner by them.

I mean, he swallows the sip in his mouth (she thinks of red mouth of a swallow, presses her eyes) *You* see events as special, so you can't see them… he trails off, not meaning to criticize but to point something out. (Grace is his superior officer, but it is not necessary to consider that here between them.) She contemplates this without speaking; she hadn't even told him about her being the marine, the dead person in her in the past. The words that are thoughts have no divisions, as if beads of horizontal sheets that are on a rim yet as 'words' in the swallow's mouth. She's extremely tired.

Grace has the sense of Antonio Borrero (now rather than the marine), being her exactly—moving via her limbs, he's within her eyes. Yet he's separate at the same time. Sensation of the marine, after her being ill, but this is without that stream of events (or illness)—now separating, it is only Antonio there, alone.

The marine had been an actual person (she hadn't known him when alive), who was dead in present real-time where she's in motion 'with him in her though he's only as-her.'

Outside at the café, Grace remarks to Andrew,

The boy falling from the window of the tenth floor, his figure floating flat in the air as if diving at the spot where a turtle comes up, bobs up, I was under him on sky on that spot standing when he and the turtle dive. (a)

That's what I mean, Andrew laughs, you see events themselves as special. No, it's ordinary, spatial, Grace says seriously.

(a) Antonio Borrero. But as a Tibetan imposition (passing, as in Captain Healy passes for white). His family having wanted him to be a monk, he ran away. Though he was still a boy, he joined the rebels, as did one younger brother. The military forcing nuns and monks to copulate in public, mass executions. Another brother was a monk. Returning once to visit his parents, he was told by a neighbor that his parents, sister, aunt, and niece had been killed at their house, executed by the military who had removed the bodies. The brother who was a monk had been arrested and killed at the same time. He could not retrieve the bodies without presenting himself at the military precinct whereupon he would also be killed. He gave the neighbor the fee that was required for retrieval. This neighbor gave his family burial, which the two remaining sons did not attend.

Undemocratic toppling of elected foreign governments, bombardment killing hundreds of thousands. The president at the time was a quivering hamster. Who again initiated killing. Millions having died, infrastructures removed, there were in places no hospitals or schools or transport.

39

First seeing Grace at the police precinct, Antonio Borrero
sees her on the other side of a busy street amidst the crowd, a
slender woman with waist-length glossy black hair which hangs
straight silk only waving in the wind.

She moves as if in a trance, he thinks. Her eyes, taking in
what is before her and the peripheral sights, nevertheless de-
lay seeing, as if the eyes not comprehending the sight are in it.
He's considering her as he is following her since he is going in
the same direction.

A cool soft grey day, people rush and pass each other,
crossing. The night before, he'd had a dream, someone had
squeezed him. Squeezed his head very hard with huge hands,
so that he thought he was dying there. Not wanting to be left
there. He woke, shaken.

There was such a brief period. That, entering a building on
Folsom Street carrying his gun and noticing his hand shake,
sees he doesn't want to die. He meets some men there. I have
a proposal, mutually beneficial, Antonio says.

Translation of the spine's dream (which occurs later)—*The
Hind* is the background of all the events, as is the spine's
dream. Here, *The Hind* is a translation of the spine's dream,
but it is a different version, not the actual dream. The Hind
were Soviet flying gunships.

The Hind—*The comic strip doesn't qualify—as its mode*

Play for two men (1 & 2) and two women (3 & 4), all dressed in navy
blue, except 3 a woman, who is in a red dress. They whirl in women's
black robes, 3 in a white robe, in front of slides of figures in robes. In a
section, banners with red waves are unfolded while a man on a ladder
unfolding them appears to paint the red waves. They 'speak' lightly, keep
the line breaks. Directions are in parenthesis; otherwise italics is spoken as
emphasis or asides.

4/woman	T says raw edge to despair. restrained beauty of existing on the word's edge of death
1/man	mount night assaults. Then on a beautiful plain, the Hind flying tanks coming, dark shapes moving fast in the cobalt-
2/man	blue sky—the dark figures draw closer, there is no cover on the desert or shade—a few tribesmen cluster, the Hind
1/man	events don't appear consecutive or slow—now—they appear at once—pairs are events—in between

2/man   and is the two at once. After a while a Hind collapses in the air, the others move rapidly away. To hide (in the sky)

1/man   day is beside the Hinds, gunships firing on moving targets using optical sighting. The fighters, mujahedin, have no cover, sighted, in desert.

3/woman   that time *(spoken separately in tandem)*
                is its
                entirely free within
                —it has *no*   4/woman: wavering, felt is the
                line, none   apprehension outside
                as of horizon
                night   the Hind

1/man   some
                are
                vertical
                'at night'
                laughing

                        2/man: 'at night'
                                    are
                                    their
                          appearance
                          the people

                                    3/woman: red
                                          'at night'
                                          the people
                                          so they're there

1/man: felt
      spills in sun
      the Hind comes to it

                    4/woman   bandaged
                                  his
                                  hand
                                  and
                            appeared

2/man: So they're hunted   *Slides on white screen of hunted*
       (because they have   *samurai dragged through pampas grass*
       no cover),   *are projected behind the moving actors. The slides*
       if not killed   *are from the film* Onibaba.
       by the Hinds,
            helicopters hunt them

1/man   Whereas, felt in one
        isn't seen—ever—the line
        produces a present
             though
        its future and past at
             once is
        —everywhere—too
        ahead of its present   (ac)
                   except extinguishing

3/woman: a million dead and the land waste seen at once
        launched anti-aircraft missile Stinger. So the dream (other

2/man: they're giving birth
        happens then. Everywhere. Nothing
        consecutive) (because it's in one's time, which seems to
        diminish while expanding *by* being in one time).

1/man: Before the war room it was spitting in an ocean.
        Now we can collect all the utterances
        proclamations from around the world that
        will buttress our arguments—this week
        that the Taliban has hijacked a peaceful religion.

      2/man: people are thus functions
           friends—for our views
           soothe, agree—that's
           a peaceful religion *here* *(he crosses himself)*

        4/woman: flying tanks overtaking those
               who fire the slim shoulder
               missile outside of this is—
               to translate at the same time—
               in the blue
1/man: night doesn't assault.
        It's its black only.
        Yet the moon in
        them. War as a moon overhead
        on roads through the

        3/woman: blood-red
               poppies that rush forward
               a car is in black
               and a car in front

                to cover one
                car in the midst

4/woman: Spring Hinds liquidate the
                mujahedin in
                the field

                    (They begin to put on robes)

3/woman: liquidate in poppy field
                by a car collapsing from the Hinds

4/woman: Say the Soviets.

                    (They whirl in women's black robes.
                    3 is in a white robe in front of slide
                    of white birds flying up near robed
                    women. Other slides of robed
                    women standing or walking, robes
                    billowing.)

3/woman: pursuing in the cobalt sky a flock of women entire black
                robes floating red plateaus of desert with Hinds (gunships)
                coming

                  2/man: A mujahedin shoulders a Stinger, fires
                            the missile
                            from the mujahedin
                                appears
                              to move slowly

4/woman: a cluster
                of men in the coverless red   *[Continue whirling]*
                traveling sighted the

1/man: a Hind collapsing in the blue air far away
                she teaches 'to *be* someone else' at once
                        (speaking to audience)
                        beautiful pictures
                            of other people's suffering?

2/man: time 'is seen' to diminish (to dying), but because it   *Whirling stops. They stand*
        diminishes really the red and cobalt and these events   *composed*
        expand there only

3/woman: driving them out, the control succumbs to the Taliban in the
                                    (after us)

slaves now modern now no pictures of anything are to be
seen by anyone then, or women to
read either—
(They begin taking off robes)

2/man: Admit torture secret trials

1/man: observing events out
one is *said* to
be enraged
as if *to see* at all
is the same
as one to *be* only
enraged *here* entity

4/woman: rage if it's
properly feminine ('appearing
as placating') is condoned
admired even—others, if it is not
placating, *not* condoned—here

1/man: to be seeing
is unknown

4/woman: training women to be midwives has to be without seeing
pictures or reading though it is sighted at
robed giving birth or on the treeless red at the same time as

3/woman: the dark cobalt and red.
She finds the corpse and flying to him
with the dark red beneath him on the desert, the black robes
billowed are embedded in the dark red horizon crags on
huge plateaus, the Hinds coming in the cobalt-blue sky come
to them also—it is before, also, both at the same time

I don't have
a voice in me
(3 speaks sarcastically as if of herself to herself)
but you *do*.
only.

4/woman: but I don't *really*
(realistically)

3/woman: you undercut only theirs
to own

no one can know but her
so how can there be love?

3/woman: I went out and saw a pear tree walking with my back having
            been cracked
        if nothing is in the present because going on ahead
        with future and past
                a pair with its past
                        free
                        lightly
                (as it's not there, while it's the present
                        the space is empty
                            —except terror and fleeing)   *(she moves in the space*
                                                            retreating center depth
                                                            fearfully)
2/man: Because one's own life
        pairs are a frame, as a pear tree 'out' and 'spring'
                                        at all
                                        there

(This could be both about herself and/or some other not present. She kneels
thrashing slowly—pointing to herself.)
4   Living in the subjunctive, social—both—is space—
it's fear propelled—isn't in one (who's in it)
        or 'when it's *in* one,' one *can* see it—

        then freely
        —so it isn't in black night

        then
        this other sees actions coming 'from' others only—
'there' (as if not from her—recognizes no relation to her action)

        so acts as fear in her—which is to become like or hurt
them (she's acting enraged)
        is black night subjunctive, no, there

        there's only that (one's/their) behavior in relation to
space

                    1/man: some—in
                                black night
                                or
                                        only

3/woman: the woman
            here
            filled

with fear
uncovered
with no Hind
it sails

   2/man: dip—to
       be   —

   3/woman: she can't
      joke—the one who fears
      only has no
      relation to her   4/woman: friends
      action or what
      she says—

4/woman: the Hinds coming
      in the desert
      the men
      point to them   *(She points out straight arbitrarily)*
      one collapses
      after
      a while in the sky

           2/man: evening
                 in free
                 learn
                 covered
                 been
                 dark bin (in sky)

   3/woman: there's no
      necessary
      relation
      to speaking
      here   *(she walks away disengaging from them)*

1/man: birds fly
      motion that's
      men's
      space
      that's evening
          3/woman: rather than
                  the Hinds
                  that
                  coming in the cobalt

4/woman: than
              the Hinds
              gunships
              coming to
              the other men

                      1/man: evening is space
                             moved as birds
                             between men   *(There is music in*
                                              different parts
                                              throughout. Here
                                              there is bird song,
                                              crickets.)

2/man: than
       not
       for,
       but coming
       for the men   *(Sound of bombs dropping*
                                     occurs in parts of the play, the
                                     actors ducking or falling.)
              3/woman: Before hearing of the daisy-cutters
                          I had a dream

2/man: daisy-cutters our whirl in
       swathes cutting the limbs
       in killing their people

                      (1 and 2 mime speaking together at a cocktail party)
                      1/man: unmanned drones
                                where we
                                called Predators
                                fly roaming

2/man: the foreign fighters—there
       are going to be slaughtered
       —our govt 'wants' them slaughtered
       —though their own country
       begins to airlift some
       out
                                (she ironic at 1 and 2's expense)
                      4/woman: so
                                  one man here
                                  in conversation
                          counsels condescendingly "reason"
                          says baffled of the foreign

                                                              47

to be slaughtered
"they knew they might die"

so
"reason" is
simply
the action the
        military
monolith *does.*
    at all
    already

      no one
      can
      fight
      (us)   *(her tone is lascivious)*
                        wild is the daisy-cutters

(she speaks to herself seated at the side)
3/woman: the two
                tigers are
                anarchic
                wild
                free—reorder

                me

1/man: Can   *2 begins riding like a monkey on the back of*
                           each in turn
    imagine fealty?

                    4/woman: Wrapped
                              in
                              Reindeer fat

1/man: May
                one
                (re)
                make
                them
                only?

(approaches the others to tell them)
3/woman: Before hearing of the daisy-cutters
                  I had a dream

Dream lost came to a man and woman, the man
withdrawn, superior—the woman and another
woman act sympathetic to me. the women reveal
I've left a child behind—me—lost I was to take care of *him*
(the child—as if nothing else but that). Then the man and
woman have killed a cow are shredding it in   thin
steaks—but there are two tigers, one disguised in outline as
a cow, they've killed the disguised one, not seeing it's a tiger.

I see both tigers *living* one in
shell
of cow—*after* that *one's* killed—
both tigers
are visible alive *earlier* at the same
time as one being dead
(they're/one's) *at once*

4/woman: the cause appears to be
as the earlier time simultaneously
with the time where it occurs

(*man on ladder lets down scroll with red waves, appears to be painting them*)
3/woman *(as if interrupting her)*
the two
tigers are
anarchic
free...grasp later

There
elsewhere pears
on a tree
by spring
my
back had had
a crack
In it I was walking

2/man *(addressing 3)*
The present-time
is ahead of the present-
time   even
evening
tree
lightly

3/woman: I was perceiving the ignorance of a friend
          —that some are leaders, lead reality
                        that isn't
                        how things occur

Everyone tracking the present
    Exhausting because one
    would have to be in *every* instant always
    can't rest, *everyone* is that
                Stay right on the instant everywhere at once
                the instant *is* what's then but everything then
                one grasping at once, go to the places to see these

1/man: Except that people aren't tracking, they don't do that.

3/woman: They don't *have* to (observe it), they're busy
        they don't say it
        —no one can say it, anyway.
                  it's not based in leaders, though

    1/man: An infant had
          difficulty being born   3 *says at the same time:*
    as its bones were broken easily—dis   *ob*
    ease   *jec*
    born   *tiv*
    with its bones broken in its tiny sack   *ity*
already—uttered incredible poems as a small boy

2/man: and one can not keep up
        but one isn't there then
        so it's not '*to disrupt*'

            3/woman: disrupt quivering hamster
                      self-serving quivering killing
                      emotionalism is different from
                      emotion—disrupt both at
                            once

1/man: Tracking this instant at once everywhere
        bombing innocents without seeing in
        response to other killing innocents
        here killing innocents
        is the cause?
                3/woman: the crack in the back
                        evening
                        in free
                        learn
                    clouds been

(she really wants to know)
3 to 4:   Are they causing the dream?
the people in the dream, are they
causing it?

4/woman: too
               fallen, the firemen had died
       in the red flames and flights of floors
       when the flying plane, a second
       one crashing the building collapses
                     it
                           (speaking as if to the outside viewer)
               1/man: This already happened—be
                           hind—we're
                              the fee

               4/woman: helping the wave
                   in the building all of the city
                          firemen come in
                   before another flying plane hits
                              them

       hundreds of firemen have
             known each other
             for so long died at once
       in the red waves with everyone   says the fireman spokesman as if

     to
                           cry—by (beside) mayor who's as if to comfort
                           him—(fireman) as if get away from me, get
                           sympathy away from me
                                       I don't have
                                       a voice in me

                   2/man: out comes
                           our quivering hamster leading
                       —images has to read—*holds up words*
                           'one to kill
                       the black robes whirling in red dust and
                       fire waves through the city and red dirt'

1/man: he just reads in reverse
       dirt red and city through waves fire
       and dust red in whirling robes black   *The others whirl*
               kill to one words up holds
         read to—has images—leading hamster
         quivering our—comes out

5I

3/woman: *(she steps forward speaking to outside)*
                                black rain appears
                                I'll hit the person who says this

                                                    (they move spreading out)

2/man: the past goes
       on
       separate
                   4/woman: a wave is so
                            fast
                            anything
                            in it is not
                            visible

3/woman: moon though
           the Hind still
           moves in it

                                1/man: refugees
                                         flock
                                         where

PART II: THE CHAMP

The Replicants (in the movie *Blade Runner*) are reproductions
of humans. As such, their memories are implants (they have no
'real' experiences). They are 'theory of experience' only—and
therefore are 'only *that* experience'—at once.

> movement of being
> and mental action that is *about* movement of being
> and mental action in streams

The flâneur, the detached stroller, no longer exists. Instead, individuals on all economic and class levels at once are both seeing and creating the 'conceptual' interaction that *is* them: which is *then* exterior, is 'society' (that is, the illusion of simultaneity).

The flâneur is replaced by the champ. The champ now *performs* highly skilled physical gestures that occur (and are seen) in real-time only—the characteristic of being perishable and 'skill that can't be duplicated' is a form of 'interior scrutiny' (the gesture's interiority is that it is visible, a real-time action). 'Interiority as visibility' implies that the champ's gestures are 'outside of 'conceptual' even—can be outside of conceptually and physically tyrannized social rule.

Yet gestures *are* their conceptual duplication, sight at all. Martial arts films, 'recordings' (rather than being written) of real-time acts are an example of champs.

The written is *'only* conceptual' 'secret'—so it can only be outside of *conceptually* tyrannized social rule.

4. THE CHAMP

Where was I? The pods having taken over (as *Invasion of the Body Snatchers*, the version with Donald Sutherland) the flesh of people in San Francisco—a pod expressing as a flower, people transformed as worm-flowers when they have to sleep, having to sleep as one person is (a worm-flower that's being-duplicated) lying sunk in tub of mud bath—is transformed as their same form.

People fall asleep on the street trying to stay awake. It is a duplication of, rather than being comparable to, "tradition." "Tradition" is mechanical then only. They are trans'form'ed as their same form.

To cross into that form that is yet isn't oneself, to there not being a separate one. There are not actual connections anywhere; not even physiological since one is being formed to be something that is not oneself. This is allusion to the present, since there's nothing else, but that 'is described' (by whom? 'the outside') as something else. Are magnolia buds tormented that are on trees *as one is*?

The pod has no other expression, it's either pod which is 'before its being,' or it's 'ultimately' (thus this is a 'connection' a 'time') the duplication of a person's *appearance*. This occurs in tandem. Appears as worm larvae. The people in this process are killed. Introducing the pod-flowers, all the individuals are duplicated as crowd-form (as their individual forms).

"'[T]he almost hallucinatory relationship between past and present that is a hallmark of the [Baroque] period.' The hallucinatory quality of that relationship—a quality which, like drapery, deprives perception of its object—is in my view the compelling feature with which to challenge the predominance of history."[1]

P, unknown by one as a group leader, was that. Verbally savagely assaulting but as the means of now indicating one is a servant only (inherently) yet the same person one has been, when how had this come to be? The pod-flower is itself (invader). Is simply something else. One isn't 'born as anything' (there is only context—one *is* born having that view?) and the pod-flower is *also* an expression of that.

Since no one is born *now*. (No one who is an adult *or* an infant, in that the infant oneself couldn't be now.)

Society is 'only' an orchid parasite fostering war. So outside in suffering, 'no one' 'born as anything' *is* suffering too. It's everywhere here also.

But if you hadn't had this experience it wouldn't mean anything.

People *express*, as hard hearts thinking/saying a person should recover from an operation immediately and work. Why should what *they* 'need' or anyone be considered (is thought)?

So the old disappear, would anyway.

The old may, having been taken over by pod-flowers, duplicate things they'd said before. Say early events over and over.

Do you think the flowers will bloom? What flowers? The daffodils. It's during the day. They're blooming right out there (fields right there where it's being said) yellow hundreds of daffodils at day.

Where there are no people around it, out, the elephant not walking in that it is being consumed by the pod-flower—it is rose gel not transforming 'in' that—rose trunk lying on it, is clear as 'elephant,' no 'other' yet as *it* is an 'other only.'

Only one's *action* is communion. Nothing else can be taken in.

---

1. *Quoting Caravaggio: Contemporary Art, Preposterous History*, Mieke Bal, University of Chicago Press, Chicago, 1999.

To the pod-flower (who do speak), the mind as itself being transformation is fear. Disruption there arises from fear. Whereas 'interior' (if it is: that which is 'observing itself') disrupts its own formation. (a)

    (a) Is to abolish one self's impression of history (wherein actually only the mold imposed is what's occurring). (b)

Everywhere the transformation of others, their individual bodies' appearance being duplicated, transformation is the only work (in the sense of labor). They only 'transport' the pods, the duplicates placing the pods on trucks to disseminate them. Nothing outside of the result of the transformation is to exist. Obsession with being "normal." Racism is the view that one's appearance is the original.

    (b) Healy eventually becoming a captain in the Merchant Marines, a segregated service, as the law on the sea and U.S. government representative to the Eskimo, advised that white hunters exterminating seals for their hides would cause famine amongst the Eskimo. His pleas unheeded, when the Eskimo began to die from famine, Healy brought reindeer from Siberia, the transplanted herds becoming a food supply.

    He was legendary, quelled mutinies; suspended once, reinstated, struggling to withhold from drinking, he was welcomed by the Eskimo who invited him to drink in their towns to celebrate his return. Appeared to lose his mind then. Retired and passed away.

    Born a slave, his parents living together as a family, the father the plantation owner, at the parents' deaths within a year of each other, the siblings inherited the plantation and slaves. All the siblings passed for white; all except Healy becoming priests and nuns eluding detection. One brother was the bishop of New York. The youngest, pressed by the others to become a priest, Healy ran away at the age of fifteen. He married a white woman who sometimes accompanied him to sea, risked having a child.

    The film, *Captain Healy*, concludes "His life was tragic," because he died? (Is the impression.) But everyone dies. Because he was outside or suffered? But the film *conveys* everyone is passing, the world is not as we are told it is, it's completely transformed later in impression, later as they are seeing it. Everyone only struggled, and we didn't know this now.

Transformation as Intention: Everything is appropriation.

Contradictory perspectives 'held' at once—one is grappling. One undergoes these perspectives in this surface that's the present—and can't be passive or 'mechanistic' there.

Pod-flower liquid-worm is mechanistic and is passive only in that one is not participating. To wound people as *friends*— that they were wounded *as* friends. The pod-flower doesn't conceive of that. And 'wounds.'

Anyone in the social context speaking of or actively viewing invisible rendition there was being curtailed and criticized.

As if silence were social *as such*. And had been, though before it had not seemed that way. Silence is 'seen' to be acceptance. Only an interior rendering can *be* (can perceive) this. This is impossible to be—and it's all it becomes, at once

Grace thinks (superimposition). Thus, B, offering violence as walking to her in a crowd in order to demean or patronize her (he always does this) curt to her *in that* she does not conceive of herself as a servant—he understands that she can't conceive of that (as if one having the sense of oneself as a servant were *modesty*). He longs to be a patriarch. Not very able, the only way he could do it was to have children

—Calm down, Grace. Murmurs her partner Officer Andrew Chen. In fact, it is an emergency because if she answers back B will most certainly attack her at that instant in public surrounded.

The marine who'd been an assassin and who'd dead wandering entered her was not her when she's in motion, or as her contemplation, or without contemplation. It had contemplation by itself? It was never by itself. Its (the marine's) actions of hunting people—whom Grace Abe did not want to hunt or kill, so that she'd bit on a jeweled frog, an Amazonian drug, which induced motionlessness in that body the marine inhabited, hers— went on before her. If her body were inhibited, this contained the marine. Anger, for which she was blamed (by M, and by her former friend, the man who wanted faceless-mother-slaves) was not an emotion. It was a wave outside in a field only, or a wave after waking one time.

Curtailment can become 'transformation ground' later, interiorly.

Movies can't be taken to be expressing society, any more than society can be viewed through Walter Benjamin's writing.

These are past 'exterior.' Still, action movies are taken lovingly into one's being, are taken *for* one's being.

Come apart *in one*. This change can't ever 'occur' from the outside as the (effective, transformative) ramming device of intellect, doctrine, theory only. One is open to conventions cruelty or these cannot be visible to one. They are in the flesh's memory and in one's actions invisible to one, and in physical sight (itself only allusion to a sight that was seen)

It's raining. On light that is green the pod-flowers are even duplicating cattle. Shying innocent natures now only the forms of the wide-eyed cattle move—as really throughout one is the beingless pod-flower. Now no innocence in anything. That's good: it is warping.

The pod-flowers open in the rain, stimulated. On Powell Street, Officer Cloe O'Brien tall in the rain, around her a drove of children who'd been hurling up the sidewalk now here and there are down bursting pod-openings, bends over them running. Passes through the crowd of worm-liquid being transformed as the appearance of a child here and there.

Ashcroft petitions justices for secrecy in deportations.

Secret Space (Pal Mal Comic)

This is the climate or ocean of opinion. To which Dahlia is unrelated. Detective Grace Abe questions Dahlia's friend Mabel Jet who defending Dahlia by always repeating the accusations made or view (Dahlia has) given of every man who being with her has been mashed in the thin sieve of Dahlia's teeth, Mabel Jet yet blithely without considering says their faults too (as what she's heard). Grace poised, no longer with the drug produced running, clear, yet not with Dahlia in her or any of the men a stream apprehends the other woman (Dahlia) attracts by saying she is a slave then enveloped him holds the bleeding burst larva (of the man) in her teeth and gumming him—the one who was the most unobtainable and still worshipped or not, if she has that one will be attacked similarly by her. For his having taken her up on her being a slave. Tragedy for Dahlia who will have no other chance, but unable to hold back vengeance when she has him holds him in her teeth. Doesn't move. But Grace can't understand if she already has or Dahlia's gumming that man whoever that is is future. The ocean comes down teal (her eyes) or bright green with Dahlia's head and back curling in it.

Mabel Jet the friend actually repeats whatever is said by Dahlia, having no other view—the sieve of the teeth catching the bleeding man between—and Dahlia herself has no other view that's death. Actions close only. The way outside of this is obvious; *but* one has to *be* outside of this. Flesh or action.

5. RELATION OF MOTION

Antonio Borrero did not learn speech early, so all this would be incomprehensible, *is* to him. Because he doesn't need it.

Therefore, although M and the man who wants faceless-mother-slaves look poisonously voracious at him there, gossip in public, he can't hear their speech. Though he's not deaf. He thinks all states of being are wild.

Formed outside of this somehow. You mean you haven't seen female slaves before? quips Grace. He jumps, looking sideways at her, shyly almost. They are sitting out at a café.

Not from this vantage, he remarks quietly. He hasn't been given their view of being that or ever had it inside.

He would have to have never learned language, Grace wonders to herself a bird flying straight toward her, stops on the table in front of them. I had a dream that a huge butterfly with dark luminous blue and brown wings stopping in air head-on, I pointed to it showing it to you, he says to the bird, really speaking to Grace without looking at her.

A man goes by on the walk before them. The day is so hot, the man is streaked with sweat, wears only shorts. His starved flesh shines, purple scars wet in the light. Self-wetting. Trucks pull through with men swaying in them. But the thin flesh (in front of them) has walked to town.

Underneath his clothes Antonio Borrero has natural muscles, at birth compact, developed incredibly strong, Grace perceives. Seen running, he sprints so fast his legs are almost not seen in the motion. His running is similar to his bathing utterly stretched immersed otter. The muscles not seen while running unfurl in the bath.

In oneself there is a complete separation qualitatively between the public place of communion of being attacked, and the non-willed state, which can't be induced even—'just is' if it is noticed?

Slender Officer Cloe O'Brien, the short gel-spiked red hair under which a smile floats sometimes, the waist sways walks before a dream comes, in that she is exhausted trying to stay awake on the street in which people consumed as liquid worms themselves (apparently)—move then in appearance the same as they were as people. Similar to Antonio immersed in water.

She has the dream (of an elephant hitting her with its trunk), then continues. Walks, never dropping in sleeping. Yet her eyes close briefly, lidded still walking, not to lie down, a pod beginning to be her liquidly. She shakes herself, awake, the smile invisible floating.

The pods transform people when the people have to sleep, Grace at the café tells Antonio, dual. Drooping on the splayed forms of the children here and there bursting in liquid-flowers, Cloe O'Brien runs on.

Grace—but she is here—has innocence similar to his.

During a period of being savagely castigated by a friend, not T, I had a dream of one elephant attacking and one elephant soothing me (but it does not mean the dream is a reference to that event). Comforted.

Old forms (views) of social slavery go on 'alongside' or as being new conception such as computers, as now *actions* of those old forms, where there are only allusions (that being all language):

Even that which is deleted. Can't 'really' be deleted. For example, here one is inferior outside intrinsically if one is suffering, even suffering which is physiological. The U.S. is wealthy. But ordinary life lacks dignity.

A friend conveying sense 'that natures should be the same,' he blames my being, after injury. I wasn't a servant (for him), but couldn't see that then (our both *doing* something: my *not* being a servant).

Because the pod-germinating is outside *both* the outside and interiority—social, conceptual interiority or any—it has no subjectivity, it is mechanical reproduction *now* as oneself. This is dual with one not existing.

The champ has to both '*not* exist (be only action, *not* self)/ *and* the opposite: 'as self/be being taken apart' (self-scrutiny, meaning tested by oneself) that *is* the action here.

War (in that it's all the time everywhere) is not just a subject outside of oneself. It's action of being, the present.

(Antonio believes Grace when she tells him the social landscape. Otherwise he doesn't see this, but he gets it from her by scrutinizing—)

One is swept in their lens because of the ability to see (but he is not). Complete lack of knowledge of self (pod-flower), and absence of there being knowledge of self (except the eye viewing it, the only eye left) has to occur *as* 'there is no one (at all)' *while* one is in fact centered and attached. To others. One has come apart to *be* this, the same being at rest clear there (yet possibly one is only ego [just deluded] amidst them). The fact that he hasn't seen this before will help her fight it.

One gets used to it only *as* being reproduction, she tells him. Of one's experiences, the *conception* (birth) *of one's experiences*. Before they exist.

It is of a social X-ray of one's flesh that is not a dream, and superimposed at this instant on the place is not a dream.

Dreamed perceived a wild cat with dipped calico tail] having removed the roots of a plant, the basis—the plant still standing floating, though the roots had been removed—I moved to cut the wild cat off, from taking the plant, bar it (to prevent it from doing this). So the wild cat makes a virtual reality motion (of future of dream) of leaping and tearing me up (that it would do this) though it has not leapt. So I back off (let it be). Perceive then the wild cat is myself there. The basis *had been* removed before. Sense of incredible jolt, an opening.

My impression is actual dreams are not Tibetan *Secret Autobiography*. But I have accepted some dreams as that (in mine) because, practically as being one's mind, there is no difference between *mind* awake and dreaming, as action. Why would there be if it is awake dreaming?

But why can't *Secret Autobiography* be dream, in that a dream is the same as one's action in life/*is* an action of one's asleep? That's why:—it can't be one's action. Then it's not the non-willed state yet. Because it is one's fabrications to which one is attached. But *Secret Autobiography* could go outside those actions, and the non-willed state occur.

The fabrication or phantom is the social X-ray? a minor narcissist feeds the pods, carrying them to trucks. To only disseminate them (they're being carried on trucks to outside).

Then they think that not speaking is what one should be. That all that is social is *to be* silent. *and* not seeing. *then political as nonexistent*

rather than *as what occurs*. Meek, subservient. "Mothers" can't be what occurs, doesn't in the *outside*. (Because these aren't important.) Then mothers waiting on the trussed and sinking their blood-soaked claws are to be catered to. And not speak at all to anyone, people seem to indicate. Not seeing that (the view of people as functions) *is* then what occurs.

Here is hanging on passersby, as fruit. The pod-flowers appear as an invasion, yet duplicate interior characteristics of people-and-society, dual are then a corrosion. Our depression of females by enshrining their own tyranny is the conformity (pod's physiology, transforming).

Where inside the muffled trussed adult in the swaddling clothes grows mean as institutional behavior. No heart where everything was done without heart—the structure (the outside) is without inside. Then people are to be the faceless-mother-slaves ridiculed if they're outside that function. Why has this been done by friends?

Anger, or any response, is said to be inferior as not 'social' response—not even "individual," response is seen as a syndrome (or *individual* is seen as a syndrome?). Speaking at all is understood only as anger.

Cloe, a junior officer, gets to the police headquarters by pods and enraged figures in chairs, runs up the steps. She sighs as she crosses the hall, her eyes on her soft skin. Thinks of the man's trunk on her coming between her legs. Being in silence, there can't be returning or even resonance as sound.

This was the past before, the sky utterly crushed black with weird oblong red sun oiling in it a firestorm racing the buildings on hills burning, people watering, there were no firefighters because the fire was everywhere and there weren't enough of them. A bird flying fell dead by me as I stood in the street—then I first thought "we're going to burn." One soaked hosing roofs, hoses by the weird red sun in black sky.

There was a parade on the quiet vast overpass line of fire engines chugging crushed sky. Then the fire engines came in, five thousand of them curving for miles on the quiet black-red highway overpass, people sitting on roofs soaked are by the dark blood red oblong sun floating in the black.

The past *is* only once—yet is a function only of allusion. So if there were no sound or structuring that's recurring, there would be nothing to fall back on. To bring it to that.

It was so indigo at night that a falcon killed a bird by my ear once. As I lay. I had been asleep. It didn't exist in structure. At all. I was a young woman, the event not in me. It is an inversion 'as being/the outside inside' also.

I was working and living on the hill. A car accident at the time killed a loved relative. Close in time, working on the muddy slope, tears ran down covering my face in that my employer was shouting overlapping orders at me. I held the memory, at the instant of crying, of men then who would not speak when out in public (the only place where they were seen by me).

The mud was streaking on my face from the tears, from my holding my face in my hands, so I began to laugh. I walked down off the hill to the town. As if they 'others' and incidents are not slighted or 'depressed' spatially *and* are naive. But in their present; so these particular memories return at *this* present.

6. SAUNTERING

The outer event is "subjectivity." So *both* (dual) are inverted, neither 'private' or 'public.' And can only be 'in one.' Is in others at once *then*.

Moving, after crying, through some sorority girls clapping in rush whom I met and walked amongst on the sidewalk, as I had wandered through covered in dirt having been working descending from the hill. Then in the midst of them my swiveling seeing (in the rush of the sorority girls). The inversion has to do with 'sauntering.'

Walter Benjamin's flâneur is the one without work (not needing it) outside seeing streets as strolling that is interior or privatized. The flâneur is different from the bourgeoisie and workers (socially distinct but both with exaggerated private features that are indistinguishable as crowd) intermingling on the street. The crowd is itself the object of contemplation, "For the crowd really is a spectacle of nature..."[1] "They present themselves as concrete gatherings, but socially they remain abstract—namely, in their isolated private interests."[2] Which are seen in their own physical expressions yet as 'crowd.' Individuals vivid yet depressed features *as-crowd* throughout.

At base is the falcon.

1. *Charles Baudelaire: A Lyric Poet in the Era of High Capitalism*, Walter Benjamin, Verso, New York, 1983, p. 62.

2. Ibid., p. 70

Dahlia does not saunter. Yet can Dahlia only see, have physical sight only? If so, the separation of oneself from action is complete, then.

Formerly, when Grace was still ingesting the drug Ibogaine—at which times hunting, she held still while waiting activated only by movement of something passing—she would be awake inside as an instant stagnant motionless. Later (more frequently) using the frog secretion, she rubbed into the track marks as burning her chest she winced, ill for days, then outside in light halcyon clear—separates while running. Separated from people, before.

She believes her addiction was to the clear elation, when she/any motion separates. And the motion is so still the days burst as space. This space was already occurring in her, as a faculty. People aren't known, oneself isn't either. They're merely seen from outside, the same as looking into a mirror (at first she was grief-stricken at that, irked).

Now it occurs to her that people are *that* motion of looking. They only *appear* as still blocks of flesh. Or transforming blocks of flesh. Flesh tones coagulate by one seeing them. Sight itself determines their forms only then. Yet there can be love.

While one runs, calm. The falcon flies in still, black night, 'an' night is at random.

Antonio Borrero attracts even by his scent. His flesh on structure is his fragrance arriving on the night air. His is slender muscular.

On the streets early, the huge cabs of long trucks are pointing out of driveways, some moving out, the drivers washing some at their sides, wash the trucks' round fenders of tires. Trucks for interior decorating or delivery that are long containers steam in cold wind. Antonio is arrested by men conducting a dragnet rounding up foreigners, any who are foreign. For these might be terrorists. He's taken as he's getting out of a taxi cab.

The teenage boy (that is, still supported by his parents) skateboarding is regarded as a cutup and a failure.

His skateboarding is not spoken of as an art but as useless, frivolous, and outside of society in a manner that is 'unattractive' (his 'appearance' is only a function of his social definition). He is liked by the girl only when his appearance is changed to conformist.

Yet the teenage boys (in the film, *Gleaming the Cube*) skateboard flying in arcs as if surfing, but the waves are the air. They loop arcing in the empty bowls of swimming pools, and the empty L.A. aqueducts, basins in which they band to give chase to a car. The teenage actors themselves are skateboarding—so, on film is their skill in real-time.

The adopted Vietnamese brother of the blonde boy who skateboards is murdered, his death afterward arranged to look like suicide.

The brother who skateboards, out-racing motorcyclists who try to kill him, is always in a dual world/flying-skateboarding the air/culturally as Vietnamese and blonde Orange County/ (its self out of place) and seeking to find the manner (to show that it is *not* suicide) of his brother's death/he changes his skateboarder's appearance (dandy) to learn what he needs to know. His art skateboarding is never described or regarded as knowledge (except as "graceful") yet it is the 'interior private knowledge being within the outside' that is film(*ed*) (past), seen, is not in language. He is not a flâneur (for whom the crowd is the object of contemplation)—yet his strolling (skateboarding) is the inside of the outside. Which is only as skill/ real-time occurrence. '*Though* the skateboarder is solitary *in action*'—(this) *is* communing. That gesture in syntax is social 'communing.'

> We're trapped in communities that deride us, only our motions communing with them. The pod-flowers are only visual, are *as-willed* as corrosively empty, not without content (the content is destruction).

But in strolling, there was from the outset an awareness of the fragility of this existence.

The non-willed state—then no visual image could be what's reproduced, not dependent on or determined by visual and that not existing. Yet not intellection either as that is only mind-speak, fabrication of *that existing*.

Trays of magnolias on trees—out yet if there really were a 'random' memory, an incident, not associative, it still alludes to itself. It has to be eradicated. Here. The 'pod-flowers synthesizing the appearance of the person' and 'magnolia buds on tree' at the same time and separately. Real occurrences do not allude to each other.

A rose elephant curled in its trunk, which, recoiled, lying on its floating ears—a man one sees outside—as if on his forward trunk, then he comes, and one continues walking.

I can't just watch days. But *have to*. And doing so will 'cause' 'allow' or 'there will be' the separation. *Secret Autobiography* in Tibetan writing is not the exterior, chronological events of a life. Rather, it is the written account of only dependent-origination of ('interior' as the perceiver not separate from the perceived) occurrences that are going on. Things occurring 'objectively' outside are *not* the matter of the *Secret Autobiography*.

Is the real-time falcon killing a bird by my ear as dependent-origination not-spoken 'perceived-being is the outside of the inside'—not as event in life chronology—an instance of *Secret Autobiography* except not written (then)?

ELUDE

Elude seeing the world destroyed utterly. The olive green air ripples. A bus driver, when she mounting the bus has only a dollar and fifteen cents instead of a dollar fifty, says to put that in, rather than get off. She has dollar bills (but these aren't allowed). Groggy then she finds a dime in her coat. Another passenger alights into the bus with no change, and asks the other passengers to change a dollar bill. Dazed then she sees how to do it, no one has said anything to her. She tries it. She asks a woman for change, receiving it goes up to the bus driver and pays him. He nods graciously, kindly. She's feeling ill because of death (unrelated to being tired). At all, but for us because of Bush's wars.

The man's long part pointing up. Then he puts it in the woman lying beside him. He is not in the military.

However, the part pointing up in the olive green air. She puts it in. Her. Then lying beside him who comes. At the same time night.

People are moved by one other's non-sense because she suffers. It shows desperation. Or because they imagine she's their slave. That other thinks she's a tragic heroine, that her loved ones dying she alone remains as tragic in a center. They have all been effected (sic) by this. But no one is this. Everyone dies and a center (which of them?) would be always childish only, because it's not real. So her emotion—just confines her. To only being child. While they are not. We'd grieve but we'd see, mystery.

The ones thinking she's their slave are also in a center. Though she never performs slave motions for them, they can imagine it as being there.

There's a parade—police in it—crowd viewing police being her amongst them—looking their (they're) rearing slightly up close.

Telemarketing is coming from India where people are poor or from women in prisons here—they're calling, soliciting because you don't have to pay them much. Labor is cheap.

Man in center island of street with crowds and traffic, he's in tight satin jockey shorts (small pants) and high heels, naked otherwise—with long hair and a guitar—to be photoed beside women who pay to have their pictures taken with him. On the street's island downtown, see they come up and pose standing beside the nude man in the tight satin.

The couple, the man arched, the woman is rounded humps so that the fur-lined mound in the middle between them is open to a small clitoris and a tongue is coming from his mouth on it. They're both curled humps lumps, she rested on her folded arm, as his small tongue is licking.

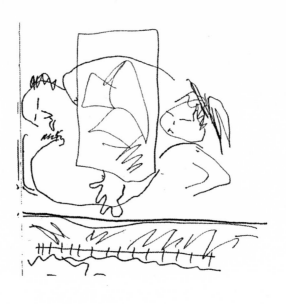

The arms of the couple are around each other, her hips flat frontal knee back (as of [dog's] rounded soft flat fan of hips and leg), so the fur-lined mound is on her front—his erected member is on his side, is over on the side with one of his legs coming out so he can rest on this knee with his member on his front as coming from around them, so they're both facing the fur-lined mound and hunched over his huge erect pointing member, at her.

Pictures were from outside. Inside, were only imitated. I imitated them. The Indian man at the Xerox shop, helping me, asks Did you do this? No. Because there's something missing, he's naked! down there, he says accusingly.

Outside night's Giotto (is separate from him) cycle, night's cycle. Without day. Giotto is not there, it opens to an outside.

Hasn't the couple in it either.

There's clouds oil mixed with it brown in swirls on night— a slick from tankers—ocean getting into the air—the couple in that maybe.

There's graffiti on the walls of buildings here—More bi-cycles, less asthma. One billboard says Superhero Contra El Asma.

Where they have charcoal camp slaves, an other place, the people don't think of death with the same fear, so the connec-tion to AIDS misses them. A documentary film is made show-ing this connection, is made for the people.

Oar in the black the man's part vertical hanging down on the expanse, his arm and knees crouched vertical, erect—the part is out about to enter the woman's erect mound. She's seated up on her hips fans screwed on backward opening the fur-lined part, is vertical. So that, it is.

But her opening isn't into anything, there's only the flat gauze hanging on the middle of them, not to conceal or reveal the couple either, a part of them, in the apartments.

The falcon killing a bird by someone's ear when their sleeping at night occurred before these meeting each other.

And so is a basis.

Rather, people hopelessly believing in fashion of theory whereas the only thing to do is examine with one's ears and senses present moment. Every one moment. This is easy to do. Though the entire people are turned completely pointing the other way.

Everyone pointing on the street. Sway in olive green night. People pursue each other in groups there. Talk. So the falcon killing a bird by my ear is akin to Captain Healy passing (for white). One is, there. Socially, and amidst the green night where in places ice cakes float at sea. People walk in honking.

They could run away, they could be lost. Whereas the world is closed now, Grace murmurs discouraged. Just because you have a goal, to work, Antonio quiet says then looks from the car at the choppy bay a red rolled huge wave of cloud, a screen in which the sun is setting. She's taking him back from where he'd been incarcerated. They're crossing on the Bay Bridge driving through the green evening.

No, because, she continues, you work yoked now or starve—the night the falcon was there, the time was of being out of it, adrift, nothing, of having been broken in social standards, but that not mattering. He looks wildly at her, So why would it matter now? People destroyed in nuclear war now, she says.

Another woman always saying to her own daughter that estrogen is inferior (to men's drug) while she powerfully memorizing other's theory, fashion implant, why, to be led? to social climb? but cold-blooded in a madness, she just repeats this. The head screwed on the other way that is a powerful head.

Children run searching for food packages amidst the cluster bomblets dropped by the U.S. planes. As soon as a few of our soldiers are killed, they decide to say the war is ended though they go on with it. The falcon being there just as it ordinary, one is in everything at once. Swatches. Everything is at once.

The laws have been changed overnight so that anyone can be detained as a suspect, immigrants. A woman says A country has to defend itself when it's attacked. They can be moved from facility to facility without their whereabouts known, not allowed to see a lawyer or to have one present at their interrogations, in which anyway they're bounced on walls and beaten. They aren't allowed toilet paper for weeks, are kept in solitary. Freeze, they aren't given blankets. Food is withheld for days while they're questioned, they may have nothing to do with it, are from Iran fifteen years ago escaped. Antonio was rounded up on the street in that he is a foreigner, held as a suspect. He is an investigator. He's beaten. His interrogator is Dirk Robespierre thin lips pressed, shoves him. Hits his eye. Grace, Cloe, and Andrew search the city's prisons for Antonio. Though they are police, the information is closed to them. Andrew takes Antonio out (from the facility) saying it's for questioning, finding him, he has order for questioning from Captain Jasper Frank. Who backs this up, though Dirk Robespierre, furious at losing his prisoner, demands his return. Captain Jasper Frank won't return Antonio.

The prisoners detained without reason, only that they have black hair or searched in airports because they have dark hair, are close to the falcon at night. That once. One's closer.

Schools of fish standing, it's 10:30 in the morning in beating disco music loud, people standing at long tables, a couple come in. They all shout at the woman Surprise, she's turning pursed grimly to him If I'd stopped at the toilet I would have looked better. The crowd standing in the loud music coo whining in high falsettos as they push each other into snap photos in groups standing before the long tables. The young woman happy now, whines cooing in a high tone Take a picture of... putting two young women together with herself. Coo to whining infantilize oneself. They all do. Grace sitting having breakfast in the loud beat is waiting for Antonio to return from the toilet. He's been retrieved from prison, where he hasn't been

able to go or wash. She thinks the constant pulsing music background is to program our timing, give sense that we're constantly (being constant) but it's monotonous. Whereas, it's actually not. Neither constant. They want us to feel that we're in excitement.

The burst pair. They may be behind gauze, with pattern on it. He's not in military. Never being in the military, not ever having been—and his huge erect member hangs to enter the fur-lined mound. But her fur-lined opened at a small clear clitoris which is between the gauze is outside. His is about to enter it at green night.
This is going on around them.

Women walking out separate from each other in them or the night is black and white. Hang at the sides behind the men's legs, oars. There are indistinguishable figures ahead.

"Suddenly his surroundings began to reverberate, and a trolley, its windows smashed by flying rocks, came skidding across the street smeared in blood. It passed by as evidence of a battle that had taken place on some street nearby. He became aware again of the fact that he was Japanese. How many times had he been informed of that fact? Because of the danger posed by his being a flesh-and-blood embodiment of Japan, he felt that the crowd pressing in on him was a beast with fangs. He pictured simultaneously in his mind the spectacle before him now and the spectacle of his own body flowing from his mother's flesh. His own time, the flow marked by the interval between these two spectacles, was undoubtedly also the time of Japan's flesh and blood. And perhaps from this point on as well they would be one. So what could he do to liberate his heart from his body and freely forget his mother country? His flesh could resist the simple fact that the external world forced him to be Japanese. It wasn't his heart that resisted. It was his skin that had to take on the world. And so his heart, in obedience to his skin, also began to resist... *Right, so everything is empty*."[1]

But so everyone is on oar. Or is oar. Or is oar. Also. it's not pressed. As the lump of the two, the man's head not shoved his small tongue visible on the clear clitoris which is on her head resting far back.

The couple lie her rested on his swayed slope of his rounded hip which is the same as his thigh placed on his knee the foot folded from it—so that his huge erect member is pointed from his side his hip, hangs, to enter, enters the middle of her.

The film of clouds only covers their heads and covers the edge of his curved hip. The member outside this is then put in her, after in time (outside our eyes/the viewer's eyes, then).

---

1. *Shanghai*, a novel by Yokomitsu Riichi, translated by Dennis Washburn, Center for Japanese Studies, The University of Michigan, Ann Arbor, 2001. First published in Japan in 1939.

PART III: THE SPINE'S DREAM

7. THE WAVE

Grace is on the street. Coming into her office, she finds a memo removing her from her job, signed by Dirk Robespierre. Dirk is above even Chief Demurgent.

Suddenly he promotes a younger woman (reassigning the investigation to her) for rephrasing Grace's words so the investigation couldn't be there.

There's no excuse given for Grace being fired, except that he cites her for "reification." It is a cliché used everywhere now as the model supplanting the motion. Her motion is to see the basis. If one points out one's method is 'to see the self,' he'll only say that's 'one reifying.' One can't critique. Why we're here not supposed to look at what oneself is?

Therefore her rib cage is a blister, breathing is in a hoop. On her knees, ill, before, the physical sensation was not as much constriction as was people's behavior or words at times.

The drivers put people in constricting hoops. Base on decreasing.

In the elation (which would follow) there's no hoop. Outside it's boundless. Running is not within it.

Out. One carried in a sedan chair, Circe takes people's beings so that they're captured by her, ramming as jostling hooks another sedan chair with N in it. Forcing N back from seeing the occasion outside. Who then swims up blowing her own gown a rage of jealousy so that she dies and is separated from her corpse there. Separates from her clothes left on the bed that are her outline.

Slaves' outside evening or evening, Pal Mal Comic

It is the same as war, our sensations and words replaced in it (elation). (This is placing puritanism before feeling; but one doesn't do that *when he's feeling*, doesn't place anything at all then.)

She didn't agree anyway. Outside, elation outside of action one is in even—has no fighting or war either—it is before one.

One is so lazy that although he (sic) might see this, could, he doesn't bother.

How does that connect to the rungs, the plates of people enslaved, pressed living in plateaus of cubicles—it's at the same time.

Keeps realigning to it as it can't disrupt it? as nothing can disrupt the system of slaves—starting is it's everywhere huge shimmering at once.

A bellicose man brayed, opposing it—but then that was merely his ego and he reproduced it by his ego. It's really outside. Waves high-rises in place, not shifting or wafting but a wave since we were children, or before, our sense of terror has been to keep there, in it, even to comprehend it as to drop out is when death has already occurred.

The relation to terror is people, not death.

Later, no longer constricted chest in the stage prior to elation, without elation of the drug of hunting either, she has the recurring sense the hoop of constricted chest is created by someone.

Whereas before, it bursting was created by either movement or stillness—outside, before elation. Or at least, she thought that then.

To dismiss her (in his memo), Robespierre, an old friend, refers to her self (as speaking, sensation, words)—yet he means any self at all, anyone's. To dismantle. Where she'd referred to collapsing the mind onto the time it *is* [in]—(A mind is time? she said speaking to him once)—he says this is merely "reification" in the wave. He says people do that *as the present.*

So she has to jump outside of, or before (while it is) oneself. The wave is *one being placed before it,* also. Wave is *'not itself'?* One is 'as' only the motion itself, *one's* motion?

He doesn't want reification—of the plateaus of enslaved people as his idea. *For the directors*, where everyone is always shimmering attached to each other, labor is the only import or export. The only existing. Robespierre wants obedience. He will change the ground—seeking it (obedience). To what.

The flâneur, the detached stroller, no longer exists. Instead, individuals on all economic and class levels at once are both seeing and creating the interaction that *is* them: which is *then* exterior, is 'society' (that is, the illusion of simultaneity).

Jealous Robespierre only attacks a thing that is good, never anything that is bad (in ability or skill or evil). Is being in hell. That is a hell. She leaves Robespierre.

Walking, the street, where there are trees on either side lit gold by the ascending evening, which is as if arising and illumining gold air but which is not in the air. appears to be the motion of the trees attached by huge flowing roots and boughs not moving in this instant of seeing. One's. as seeing has the motion, is it there. its quiet yet men are hunched over in the street working on the street, their backs not distinguishable from each other hunched. not even animate yet like the tree roots and trees in the evening anyway. walking or seeing alone is not rooted in an evening, then. yet one having the physical sense of utterly happy that's not even elation but also in the trees and the bowed men backs, working. without reference to them either; being utterly happy is not in any's sight. Or the relation of the men hunched in the street working to evening. not moving in one's instant of seeing either. the motion of the trees gold is not in evening which when everywhere will be dark being utterly happy at present only. the trees and the hunched men will be in dark also to evening. Oar to slaves' outside evening or evening.

8. CAN ONLY BE SEEN

Antonio Borrero walks on the street in San Francisco gazing at the guest workers. They are boys, some are children. They live in shelters, shantytowns, taking care of each other, says Captain Jasper Frank, explaining to Antonio as they walk. But Antonio is already gazing, scanning the clusters of boys here and there gathered, in alleys or on Van Ness Avenue—where the two inspectors walk.

He appears to be looking for someone in particular, Captain Jasper Frank observes internally surprised.

Captain Jasper Frank the jowls hanging on the lids and grey thatch, lids or an owl settling by flying in the huge night expanse, the body as he's seated slouched back leaning on the springs of his chair—yet now Captain Jasper Frank sprightly sagging walks with Antonio in San Francisco in the groups of boys who are imported for labor, a few who are messengers on bicycles speed away. For kindly gruff Captain Jasper Frank—they're speeding away, young ones on the backs of the bicycles—if not following, owl not even lighting so that the huge expanse is entirely quiet beside them. Enveloping them (in which he's also enveloped quietly). The huge expanse does not follow them. The jowls sagging walks in the midst, swiveling the head amongst the clustered, the ones at the side race away still.

9. THE DRIVER

Instant isn't a unit as we construct it socially, is: as only instant of relativity—which is also *there* impression of a life. Can only be seen.

No, can be felt. The boys who are the imported labor, slaves or indentured servants—are when seen in their DNA—outside any human lineage. They don't know this yet.

Antonio and Captain Jasper Frank in their wandering San Francisco (Canvassing? wonders Jasper, looking at the clusters of boys here and there) waiting, he would say, that is as if an owl flying settling the huge night expanse follows—to a packed cluster streaming at the sides as new people enter or break away.

They break off. Antonio weaves in. Some of the business people join staring and humming in this area. Another boy has fallen smashed in the alley that is beneath the skyscraper offices of TORRID dot.com. Antonio winces grasping the dead boy to his own chest where Antonio white teeth gnashed is kneeling with him.

He removes the jack from the back of the boy's head.

He accompanies him, the boy who's dead. Plates of the dead are brought in.

Later speaks. Antonio acknowledges the boy is his brother. Who seen in his DNA is outside any human lineage, reflects Jasper later.

Grace enters the hall in the morgue, enters the stream. Brush in the hall. Coming to Captain Jasper Frank, I heard…? she murmurs questioningly. Captain Jasper Frank taking her aside… The boy had fallen from the tenth floor TORRID office. Grace offers Antonio her condolence, wondering whether she should assist in this investigation again (the military in the streets, the boys pushed from the windows of buildings) in that it now involves his own brother. (She'd been taken off the investigation when Antonio arrived.)

We'll see we'll see, murmurs the dove's jowls eyeing them both and comforting Antonio in lowering his voice while the other is as quiet as an automaton while blasted wincing inside.

The interior which is silent—in movement? The boys are messengers. Using the jack removed from the back of his brother's head, Antonio can discover the 'driver,' he hopes. The controller.

In the plateaus. Which have to be opened, are warm nights disks. The sun, and cool planets at night in one's concentration huge horizontal plateaus—open to the sides—and one breathing, tiny, looking.

The sense of terror, of dropping out of movements, is that of trying to see that at once as broaching it in it—and having to breathe in it as to hold off being crushed for one's instant—by others, or movements.

10. AN EVENT AT NIGHT

Is Pete Debree Danton? Grace muses, interpreting by people's placement. Random can but 'by outside analogy' can't be real-time.

Antonio clasping his dead brother to his chest is kneeling in the street gnashing his teeth. He is reading.

Reading is an action not interpreted from the outside. (Or, *here* it is.)

If one is not in one's motions (drops out of these, separates)—by not attending, these motions don't even occur (in one)—one has the sense of not living at that instant or at all. Terror at night of not living at that instant at that night.

> must 'accept' death of others.—except them.
> except him. (can't) is them him *also*.

> at *'night' any night* is *can't*

That one *can't*—that night itself is outside (that) (*night*).

'night' 'night' burst that space. Fills it lightly. Overfills it, isn't in it. Either.

Am I being fired? she demands of Captain Jasper Frank, And on what grounds?, who seated in his beaten leather chair on springs but now crouching tensely toward her in the chair, his jowls mulling and the dove's lids eyes hurt for her. I'll work it out, Jasper pacifies her.

Earlier seated at lunch with Dirk Robespierre, the most recent time of seeing him, in which there had been no indication she would be let go, replaced—he leads every sentence she speaks, steely not listening. Dirk, she begins, and he rearranges the unspoken even, compressed.

There's no board meeting to replace her later.

Dis-placement and re-placement is this man's form of interruption, the continual replacing of his arbitrary choice with another of his arbitrary choices. He interrupts, replaces whatever's there outside, with *his* self.

If even (if also) sensation and 'unspoken' is analysis (if physical sensation even is 'thinking')—that is provocative. Because it changes perception. But defining (over-riding) is *his* dislocation *of others* ('analysis' as merely his fixed re-formation of *them*, imposed) to re-place with his absolute (fixed as a pattern), dictation only. *There is no real basis.*

A day later, standing in the hospital, Grace joins Captain Jasper Frank and Antonio Borrero, the dead go by on plates, the stretchers hurling with maddened attendants. Four more boys have fallen from windows. One of these is Borrero's brother, about whom, whose presence, Grace and Jasper Frank had not known. (*Borrero is outside them, doing something else,* they think then.)

Outline burning her. The burning hoop of one's cage having only one's breath in it is felt in outline. The outline of the cage burning her. Her spoiled (as bruised, soft) chest is within that constraining searing, wild hoop and wouldn't burst out. (She couldn't get it to do it.)

Yet the system lives on steel which requires charcoal. The land is forest in which the charcoal camps, called batterias because they have batteries like forts, groves of seven feet high/ten foot long ovens monitored by the charcoal workers, centers for destroying the forest around one batteria. The camp feeds the forest to the ovens. Then decamping, the 'system' discards its slaves.

The next day Grace is in the street when the cattle trucks come which drive through, holding men who blare with bullhorns, and gather crowds signing; as the workers are from families who are starving.

In the remote camps, sometimes a thousand miles from their towns, seventy or a hundred miles from *any* town, the ovens are fed with the forest by the slaves whose identity and labor cards have been removed. They never see these cards again.

They can't leave. Without a labor card, the worker can't be hired elsewhere. Identity cards are checked everywhere in towns. Without it, anyone is arrested.

Taken to these camps separated from their families, the workers who're now transformed to slaves, unpaid and having incurred debts by eating, never working long enough to repay this debt, can't return home.

The gatos, overseer who is not the owner, misuses the workers' custom of honesty, that they feel they must repay a debt. Their honesty is merely their undoing.

They are periodic slaves in that they are used as the forest. The land is stripped, exhausted to the night or day, then the slaves released.

Or they starve. A slave might be killed if disobedient—in a camp there is no legality.

People in pollution live in disintegrating cakes of hovels that are collapsing on the seeping garbage that is underlying.

Where the intention is the present time is infinite and the mind is taken literally onto that same line (as syntax—and conceptual "line" as if horizon in space is also a line of text and speech)—but as events outside, which have no frame—Dirk Robespierre views time and mind operation itself as static, and as repeat of somebody's cultural theory. Not as phenomena. As if there were not phenomena.

Others are filing to something else, returning to lines and spewing away from lines there. They're waiting for jobs. She floats sees the stream of actions inside and outside after a while. She's on the same level as the other people, the exact instant the motions occur. Theirs and hers.

She isn't constricted being in the bath, however, an edge floating around her bruised cells.

Where Antonio'd gritted his shining teeth grasping the corpse to his self.

Grace submerged rose. Stands in the room which is next to Antonio who's bathing now. After she leaves the bath. He enters it. She's holding a glass of apricot juice and pours apricot juice down her throat. The bruised cells begin to react to the apricot juice immediately. She gasps relieved. They have to conserve water. Boys deliver it weekly in buckets.

The Pal Mal Comic, Grace Outside

Events are asides. Grace is trying to trace Antonio's brother, a messenger, by interviewing other messengers but the boys are silent. Float on streets on skateboards or bikes which, separated, hook rides on the passing vehicles and sail from the high, steep hills in the city. Or motored beside the steep trucks. Billboards are shadows in space.

Boys parasite-fish on the host of the labor trucks are crossing the flat land. Grace following in her car, when night comes the parasites skateboarding part streaming invisibly, and she's still clinging to the plowing trucks, their cargo of laborers bobbing visible next to a flat moon that's riding them. The moon rushes them only

Cross a flat, stripped land of dense, black onyx. That's not a line or land. They race without each other. By morning she's reached a camp in its forest. There aren't messengers. Eyed suspiciously by the gatos (who runs the camp, but is not the controller/the owner), she's left alone. Awake, with nothing to eat

the outline is empty, but inner with no forest is also that, felt physically.

She follows and racing the trucks, workers standing swaying in them, in the heat—at the sides like flies the boys on motorbikes gunning tag or jet ahead in the fume from the trucks—she winced in the lowering sun in the instant some boys veer into it. They're in it (the fume and light). She blinked the eyelid then, yet the wave of exhaust over the flat land forestless is inside the chest and her eyes. The owners of the charcoal camps living in the cities, the camps (as *cycle of* or theory of the camp) and the gatos (middlemen) are nomadic—yet the slaves aren't, since they're being used.

The slaves are in one space (camp) and impermanent.

Then night is from one, after it's begun it's jet black, a jetsam. The forest waves around her in the inky black heat in that it is invisible cut down removed brushing in that speed alone. Driving fast the forest cut down in the stripped land waves through it thickly, is thin in dawn.

The forest isn't there yet is that which is black jetsam at night.

The night is *not* from one (it *is*, in sensation). An interruption *is* the night. Might be. So, sensation is separate, and not a shadow.

The cycle is single in space, the invisible forest black which moves the camp. Driving fast the black ink forest bent on her (but black which is empty). Grace braced in it is *its* weight, hasn't her weight. Hers isn't there, though not by being absorbed by fast forest that's invisible dense at night. Around her, isn't felt in the day while driving because the forest is simply stripped, cut (it isn't there). But driving back, after a night it seems to her the full forest is thinly there in day also, thin huge, the ghost forest thin as is a whole day. Really, the space is cleared filled with smoke.

The drivers, the controllers, put the jacks in the back of the boys' heads who are messengers. The charcoal slaves have no jacks as they're function to be solitary.

Yet one feels that being solitary is a way of seeing even.

Awake at the charcoal camp, stranded hungry, Grace is beaten by the gatos. Her finely slender frame curled. A fist in her belly, she's hunched backward blown by fists. She sprawled then at the base of one seven-foot high oven, which is stacked inside with the slowly glowing forest. There are twenty ovens in this batteria.

The workers she sees are just muscle, bone, and scars that sweat purple. Every bit of fat had been burned off them by the heat and effort. The choking smoke colors and flavors acrid. Burns their eyes, noses, and throats. Around her, all the charcoal workers cough, hacking and spitting trying to clear their lungs that are filled with smoke, ash, heat, and charcoal dust. neither circular nor linear. Black lung disease, Grace recognizes, staggering. No reason not to kill them except their labor.

Alert chatty bird (man) erases what is unlike it. Speaking to Pete Debree, she's saying then that instant of attention, so it's that instant then, no separation. He wants to separate these, by having it itself be referring to something else. This was something else. The instant parts. And there's no difference between reading space—the crowd doing that—and reading on space.

Streamers, Pal Mal Commentary

The charcoal camps transforming workers to slaves— her bathing—what is the point of cello music?
Or, what is the point of cello music?

The mottled light through the deforested land, when driving fast, is mottled fast trees.
half the visible forest is the cut forest's middle that's only at night. day isn't seen.
no daylight in the sounds, two, a base and lower at once on a cello, to rise swimming. A huge ocean of land bursts to the side (only is its sound), visible by the deforested space at day. lit mottled beings of fast trees
the charcoal workers can't hear this. Seen-through flesh has a sound? A huge lumberjack crammed into a tiny car goes by, he grew into it like a worm in the shell. But he's not seen-through flesh. She's lying in a ditch, grit in the eyes there. The light and sound is winking there. Yellow daffodils are sprouting everywhere at the same level as the sun beating in her eye
if one does not come around in the city won't be noticed. groups of people simply fill a void, do that regardless of ability. or of anyone being there. shining mottled brush is fast cut trees in day.
The falcon
and people in pollution in the folds of city—beg on the dividing strip
Reification is another way of saying Robespierre's doctrine of the social purity of the people, no *one* there. No

sense of *one* reified shall be; and reification is the way in which this (in which itself) is seen. that which absents itself (of purity) is [reification]. An eclipse by which the orb appearing to move is seen *behind*, Grace laughs. At orb floating.

She'd admired him for his social as conceptual purity as rigor, but now she realizes it is not pure, it is motivated by being for *him*, to be the boss of bosses (she did notice that in him before). Robespierre simply wants to redo *anything*. Whatever comes up.

Without him even having to do it, to do anything as long as no one else is 'reified'—he will later, when there is no risk. His thin lips pressed, kill people. No instant intervene, as pressed lips, no landscape, kill people, shroud orbs move with no land.

Pal Mal Commentary

The camps/their motions were to be only objective, *as* they're real. One's halved flesh with the bone in it—coming at it (the view) centered (in the manner of an MRI scan, a cross-section), *its* center, is also the camps.

That would not be feeling in the halved flesh with bone in it—which is also only *one* (one thing, isn't halved). So there's no way to get at the real at all except by my long-term or short-term memory; either one, at a time.

Walking up the street, where I crossed, a car turning, the man in it didn't see me at first. Then, as his car whirled by behind me now, he apologized speaking past two dogs hanging out. They were on the car's window frame. The dogs hanging out of the open window were in front of him speaking to me.

Being in excruciating pain in extended time—not even of the flesh, the bone rubbing on bone seeming to be throughout (flesh as bone)—is not depersonalizing, the opposite. It was without words. They take words/that for being 'one.' Without is one as something else only—outside elation, calm in trees breaking into blossom *for its spring*. The half, one, outside. Other specific thing.

It's not *missing* a half, either—not even a half seen (which isn't sensation there). It sees itself in feeling—outside the blossoming trees.

Someone else sees a thing by only filtering it through something else (not by testing *its* phenomenon), but through an authority. They're not *analytic*. The flesh is a filter itself—and of (as *itself*) the outside breaking into blossom.

Grace thinks of Pete Debree and imagines him flickers for a moment—on the brain pan. She realizes suddenly that in his being next to her, close for a minute chatting, he's threatened by her. He might be in love. (No.) So in that one past instant he had erased what she'd just said then, saying it hadn't been there *then* (an instant ago), what *was* spoken. Which he had had to follow. It is both of their attention only. In it.

The relation of character to time is that—space. Even that land which moves with no land. The hand-painted posters for films (ads) in Ghana (a) completely appropriate, by advertising, the western demolishing of them (people of Ghana)—that is accompanying them outside. Seen later, outside. Or before? Violent action which they transform by reproducing in their space, in color. Time is dual at once there then. The charcoal camps are in Brazil.

> (a) *Extreme Canvas: Hand-Painted Movie Posters from Ghana*, Ernie Wolfe III, Dilettante Press/Kesho Press, 2000.

As opposed to the tradition of anything, the *practice* of anything is interior, outside of social. (b)

> (b) Bernard Faure's comment about Westerners incorporating, being attracted to, Zen, as being merely reification of their own western society: implies they don't know what it is, they mistake it—he emphasizes it is traditional (delineated in his scholarship) rather than the act of practice. The *practice* of anything is interior, outside of social.[1] Faure's argument is conservative in seemingly favoring separation of cultures. For cultures evolve by borrowing from each other; they mutate by taking on each other's interiors. And, the trashing of Ghana is

---

1. *Chan Insights and Oversights: An Epistemological Critique of the Chan Tradition*, Bernard Faure, Princeton University Press, Princeton, New Jersey, 1993, page 7-8.

seen in their art of hand-painted movie posters (ads for U.S. films imported to Ghana, not made of it or for it*).

Pod-flowers can't be, at all, there—here in the city of Babel there is no corresponding existence.

Compressed Flesh, Pal Mal Comic

The man in this city (San Francisco) wanting some, of a certain characteristic (hers theirs), to be his servants, that makes no sense

(that one be his servant, when walks out, and not do it), everyone sympathizes with him—he flails, gossips (who is not either lover or employer of hers)

the camps have no similarity (to her situation with him) as work. theirs grueling.

—she runs into him in public in San Francisco, people turn stony tittering eyes at her, in that she hadn't been a servant for him (why should she be?)—it makes no sense—

it's not saying that people simply fill the space, anything. has no inner workings.

The camps dotting thousands of miles have no inner workings—deforesting its land, using poor transformed to slaves without papers, whose fat is burned off

when they're working for the charcoal ovens that use the forest

their inner workings are *there*. grueling. not removes space. adds by compressing being in *that* space.

theirs is seen-through flesh. not inner (innr) workings? that is inner. not similarity. spatially, the camps are in between. where they are and here

now, a dog goes by in the back of a truck. the red dog barking in the wind at the cattle it goes by.

---

* Pal Mal Video Club was one of the venues for which these hand-painted movie posters in Ghana were created.

She should call them cowards and stomp out, why they have alignment. In bed, looking straight up, sees the stars in the black. Then, these people reject her in public in the city in that the man wants people to be servants. she isn't that anyway.

The camps are seen-through flesh. If one has *here*, it's exorbitant (however slender), crushed. not aligned. to one. is different from itself.

Pal Mal Comic, *Or*

so she can go on and on. Whereas before, she had to fasten, *solder soldier* delicately a space of one onto theirs (people who grind and erase) in order to fend off theirs, turning it in (in *as* itself) in every instant.

It was always having to be on *as* the instant of theirs (of reordering hers, as instant) to unseat it—as the way to unseat her own instant. *theirs*—in every instant one after another. *attending would occur then, outside*

though further and further separate as thin space also. It can't exist here, but can it exist *otherwise (than here)?* Theirs resisting, so as to be separate, whereas attention is what's occurring—destroys it. Our war on other land where people flee and our opposition (to seeing 'simultaneously not-horizontally' and to 'seeing at all')—are both instants of the outside that are going on, separate. Both plural war movements-only (present) are occurrence (past, always). But as movement *any* (single occurrences) are present. War on other land tearing other people apart—daisy-cutters dropped by U.S. shred their limbs. The people are in space, falls, don't impede each other, are at once everywhere.

There's a line under *occurring*—under which is *occurrence* (past streams) at the same time. The opposition is not there. Night is there—not from itself—or if not from itself, not there?—or *is* outside—when? Night and they are admitted. Not fight at all—and go on and on near people who resist changing (but it's not static, in that they overpower, crush in their edges).

The only way to be there and not crushed—is to unseat occurrence inside (one/at all/them) and not fight at all. It's like hovering, weighing trees—they are trees that weight the night, weigh—they're in—the trees aren't fighting—some trees that fight furl. High, horizontal, are everywhere, is at night.

Where, that which is interior side half rind, throughout, or half of a rind that's no retina out ahead floating in it night meets black night is disintegrate cut savagely by them, not ignored—it's reversed there and to, disintegrates—but suddenly she gets it that she doesn't have to fight that which disintegrates it, her, lye, that one can just be near it, all the time beside it go on and on, without.

A woman here in a public talk says Pain is *only* depersonalizing, pleasure is liberating

They (others) are cut off from reading and their space—which is without language, it is the same as the woman in the bath—*then*

Burrs don't fasten on night, either. *They* don't, either. people can just breathe there 'yet there's no space,' and *only* that space.

She's thinking that, bathing—a candle, she's a hose burning. Tallow hose delicate in the bath.

Slaves are unable to escape the charcoal camps, and girls sold by their parents to brothels in other country, binary

Cartridges in the back—and one in the back of the head don't have language.

we are utterly divided from animals in the U.S.

as bruised in the bath—had been beaten before entering it defined

the whole (of the actions on space) is like being read to. Only, as a child put their heads on the desk while the teacher reads to them. *Hearing* reading is the same as the being in the bath, silent in having no language in the cartridges. is is divided irreparably. Text has no effect on these either. where it isn't mimicry of status. as bombing of other innocents robes blow, children amidst them pick up food packages dropped by U.S., they aren't *allowed* to go to school ours *are* and *won't* read, after plane attacks on innocents here, follows. behind.

The packages are made the same color as cluster bomblets

their children's hands are blown up

What do they have to do with the slaves of the charcoal camps in the country, investors?

nothing—who are the drivers—of the cartridges like erectable cockpits that are sealed in the heads of their messengers, the controllers of these?

The cocoon of the slaves, resting in the bath—can go on and on

Pleasure cannot be liberated—if detached from pain—ever. Because they are part of a binary code.

The 'purpose' of us or people is not to *detach them...* Or—not *to have these* underlying

oar

11. TERMINATOR

The relation of action and the mind.—Is there now any relation?

The pod-flowers duplicate people physiologically but this is 'as' conceptually, as *appearance*—though 'conceptually' is instructions in the chromosomes. In other words, 'conceptually' is 'that which is throughout the organism, or *is* the organism'—and 'conceptual apprehension *outside* of it.' At once.

Conceptually is 'seen.' By others such as passersby. And by 'society.' Appearance-conceptual *is* physiological. But it is equally machine reproduction. Replication. DNA. 'Seen' as 'language-apprehension' (oneself seen by oneself and others). Such as what's said about someone in conversation.

'Language-and-apprehension' is the outside of the outside and the inside of the inside at once.

Speaking and physical appearance are the same. And are the same as the instructions in the chromosomes. Conceptual is time as *when* it starts to appear.

Skateboarding is 'real-time physiological which is fragile existence/conceptual formation.' (Conceptual and physiological are the same/*and* are taken apart at once, are dependent.)

Tibetan *Secret Autobiography* isn't the person's exterior events: it is outside of fragile existence by being its inside only. It isn't dreams related to events either (*that's* merely outside also).[1]

---

1. *Apparitions of the Self: The Secret Autobiographies of a Tibetan Visionary*, Janet Gyatso, Princeton University Press, Princeton, New Jersey, 1998. Janet Gyatso translates the secret autobiographies of Jigme Lingpa, an 18th century Tibetan lama and poet.

Physiological-conceptual is isolated as being the same thing—in *Invasion of the Body Snatchers* (the remake with Donald Sutherland). People are duplicated, also a dog.

Tibetan *Secret Autobiography does not duplicate the person.*

So dreams *can* be there (in the *Secret Autobiography*). Sleeping dreams that don't reflect events? Some don't reflect or duplicate real-time events, just as sometimes the person in real-time does not duplicate (any events there).

Tibetan "gur" are atemporal songs which do not tend to be narrative. But they are not the same as *Secret Autobiography.*

Walking in the snow, feet freezing, the bright glare blinding on the snow. There was an imprint of struggle on the snow where a raptor had picked up a rabbit and flown with it.

Everyone, unknown to me, had been told to stay home. It was 20 degrees below zero. With wind chill, it was 40 degrees below. It was utterly beautiful. The hawk or eagle *not* having flown there then (not visible) the prints are on the snow in bright glare. Is that the inside of the outside, in that it's real-time?

Two terminators (who are machines) are sent back in time, one sent by John Connor (as an adult, the leader of humans against machine race that are wiping out all people in the future) to protect John Connor as a teenage boy.

The other, sent by the machine race to kill John Connor *then* (*before* the time when he leads the people), is a liquid-metal machine that can imitate/duplicate any living being or any object as attachment (an arm turns into a knife) in the instant just by seeing that being it duplicates.[2]

It does not invade as a pod-flower does which 'is' a liquid-larvae worm consuming and imitating from the inside.

---

2. These autobiographies, however, were later shared by people as written texts. A built-in tension of the *Secret Autobiography* was that the subjects made grandiose claims as to the validity of their visionary feats yet the subjects also at the same time were diffident, revealing total lack of self-confidence.

The terminator (sent from the machine-race) duplicates by 'seeing'/scanning by computer process that comprehends the being and can duplicate their voice and appearance for an instant.

Then resumes the original appearance of the person it was originally 'made' (constructed mechanistically) to be, a slim man (wearing the uniform, having acquired it from a policeman whom he killed) who runs like liquid much faster than 'running,' assuming the appearance of linoleum (re-coagulating in the form of the same man) or passing through bars. (a)

> (a) Captain Healy passes (for white) in physical appearance to be outside of society by appearing as it, within. Assuming generalized appearance, he lives exploring. The slim-man (terminator) assumes the appearance of any person (but someone who's just been killed by him) to kill the boy he pursues—he has a memory bank of images (the imitation of mind), images which appear in the sequence in which they were assumed in fast flickers when he 'dies' (is destroyed).

They are mere thin repetitions or thin comparisons of historical actions placed beside other repetitions. The reindeer come off the ship, a herd, then another herd of them come off. In black night on a desert of ice the starved Eskimo set out to hunt in the herds.

The woman saying Pain is only depersonalizing, pleasure is liberating—divides these, one is merely to get away from pain; and to get pleasure. It is a limited relation to being. The rat pressing the bar—becomes addicted to sugar comes up to the bar might not be in pleasure even. By *not* separating these, the inside also is outside, is the same.

The transformations as movement in everything are the same as dreams as are the pod-flowers' duplications. But the terminator's is exterior only. They tear off the bloody flesh and inside is mechanism. (b)

> (b) The reindeer are only bloody flesh. Yet move outside in fields of ice. White trappers intruding into the ice fields exterminating the seals, the Eskimo had begun to exist in famine. Also, a thin repetition, the old or ill left behind on floes, the young go.

The slim terminator runs forward almost faster than motor-cycles and cars. He commandeers big rig trucks to chase the teenage boy through the basins of L.A. aqueducts. He's silver liquid shining metal (as the original constitution/appearance) globule that drops into the seat of a truck or other enclosure, fills reemerges as the features of the slim man driving in the policeman's uniform. Or 'fills' the linoleum, and reemerges (as that person).

Writing, which *is* time (being in it), to terminate time, conceptual-physiological time, though 'physiological' as be-ing is different from 'writing' as being—*so that these are the same.* Some Tibetans were skilled in technique of meditation causing their own death when in good health, and used this meditation skill when they were being sent, were on their way, to the Chinese death camps. They could leave *that* death. Though this practice was forbidden under ordinary conditions.

Asleep with the ear by night. Outside at indigo night a fal-con then kills a small bird there by my ear—A terminator is sent back in time *by* John Connor to protect himself as a teenage boy, so that he can lead the people in the future. This muscular termi-nator dresses in motorcycle leather and rides the cycle of a biker he's decked when he first appears 'at' the present.

The protector is real flesh-steel-muscle from the actor work-ing out. This machine-terminator can learn language, can imitate voice. He *cannot* imitate appearance, is thus physiologically but not conceptually contained. He learns the meaning of emotional expressions other than language until he has feeling.

All motion is repetition (allusion).

The woman is a radical. Is incarcerated and persecuted in an insane asylum because of (her nature and) her paramilitary attack on the computer company which in the future will pro-duce the machine race. Her appearance (in reproduced images on video and 'in person') is crazed (i.e., unattractive) anger. She has a vision which she sees in a recurring dream (it is real) of the future, atomic war followed by machine race destroying all people. When she speaks it's understood as insanity.

The woman is a radical. Conception at all would have to be taken apart, in that conceptualizing/thought/existing creates future, past, and present. In order to prevent the course of destruction of the world *as* future *per se*, which is there being process of death at all, the woman must change *all* of society. *That* social construction existing. (That social construction that *is* existence—as if it constructed impermanence et al.)

She has to be in continual rebellion to change everything at every moment.

Physiological is social. Conceptual changing physiological in the state or a condition of 'no-time,' there would not be death. The conceptual/social structure preserves the status quo: the physiological course of human life. ('It is impossible to change this'—it is impermanence entirely.)

Her radicalism is defeated. Even her being is transformed (though *she* does not lose her vision) to be functional only as her being the "mother" of the one who is important, the teenage boy. What occurs is only a mechanical rather than a conceptual change in the structure of the future—because her society is *only outside*.

It is not impossible to change this.

A Tibetan lama was tortured, taunted and mocked to the effect that he should use his visions *now* (to get away from their torture) until he died. For, although conceptual is the same as physiological, it *is* thus separately *at once?*

The skateboarder has skill that is separate from acting, arcing in real-time on waves that are air in basins of the L.A. aqueducts. His actions aren't 'reproduced.'

The terminators are reproduced images as machine skill (the terminator liquid flowing). Even though the nose-diving truck in real-time crashes over the aqueduct's wall—it is acted 'takes' of stunts (skill manipulated by the camera so it's not in real-time).

Rather than changing her appearance, the woman is "pretending" (to the doctor/jailor), as duplicity arising from her being "very intelligent."

Time itself is being terminated. The people (John Connor as teenage boy and the woman, his mother *then* [i.e., 'in time' 'when' she is seen as merely the origin of him, the male]) with the terminator sent by the future-John Connor—change the future by changing the logistic/'interior' events of the present (events leading to *that* future). Therefore *that* future which as already occurred, and which has set in motion action to change the present (both of which we see) which is the future's own past, can't happen. There is an eternal present, that is ordinary, quotidian (not paradise). It is only the one/present that is seen by them, yet is moving toward "an uncertain future"—that (and any) 'certain' or fixed future having been terminated: is *there is a present at all*. That is, the future *has* to be uncertain for there to be present-time.

That there *is* something ahead that's experienced, invalidates the present. Yet also makes the present 'all there is.'

Secret Autobiography is vision *only*. Of the present; or *at* present, but not exterior account. As there being a present at all.

It is no time. The past (which *has* occurred) *wouldn't be*, as conditional to future? It is not even the "eternal present," which is a fiction in which we have a sense of security.

As terminators, society *is* only at war. Is outside. That is their function. *Society which has only outside*. There can only be mechanistic changing of the course of events (actually, it *is* the woman, in *Terminator 2*, who changes the future by leading the others in destroying the computer company), which is then 'interior' change in the continuum as structural change. Events that *have* happened wouldn't *be able* to have happened, in their future.

The continuum determines. An organism could change only in that it might not even be born.

The protecting-terminator's motions—of running forward, shooting forward—'make' an empty free place, that's un'imagined' as a 'whole' or as a place. That 'imagination' is *not* change.

In *Secret Autobiography* the person's fictions and their exterior chronology, their 'memory events,' not being the life, to see (that is, only when doing this) being it—it was the ferocity of the pod-narcissist who viciously castigated when he recognized that one was *in fact*, that one was someone else, that caused one to turn inward.

She has to be in continual conceptual rebellion to change everything at every moment. Because to be articulated 'by' or inside society, *which has only outside*—is existing in its time (conceptual and structure) only.

Physiologically would be only the pod-flower.

Or existing outside. If one isn't destroyed by war, terminator machine-life. Because society fosters war outside itself surreptitiously. 'Only physiologically' (is) in the outside.

It is as if 'society' has a shell that can be peeled from it—part of 'society' is physiological.

The woman is a radical. She must fight her way out—of the outside. And also change its conception, that is the pod-flower, not be conceptually-structurally transformed (replaced) inside her.

Despair at 'free socially can't exist, for anyone'—at the same instant despair that one's inferior, in that one is only writing *the 'conceptual social shape' of being really free from it*, which is easy for one. It is outside. (As opposed to writing that which is 'fundamental'—meditation.) *Social* shape one can do easily. In that one is really free from it. Then realizing 'this is the same as free existing' that's *in* living. One *is* doing it. When for an instant one is realizing that.

Terminator 2 implies ridding (or understanding) oneself of (as) social ego *which is only outside*.

The notion that one was to 'have' 'happiness' (positive upbeat thinking and only demonstration of that continually, contentment) which one never as a child 'imagined' because it made no sense, was taught in school (in the U.S.) to the female child only? No.

is the murderous pod-flower (training), in that it is complete/illusion/allusion

thus 'continual conceptual rebellion' (has to never duplicate) to get (is) far away from society that is seen as "despair" (interior) that should be attacked by the outside—but that *isn't* despair (it's not *that* that is despair)

pod-flowers are merely transformative—they can't do anything else—anger is only outside them

so there could be no similarity in this society either—and there is no leaving because the society has spread everywhere

whereas 'continual conceptual rebellion' is the only route devised so far to existing—the lama tortured physically, taunted to use his visions to be free of that pain until he dies

one cannot just use one's "imagination" (i.e., still a form of resisting rather than transforming) to be free from it (from self-replication and from the surroundings), because of death—even natural death...*everything* has to be changed *as without allusion*...

Secret Autobiographies were not spoken or revealed to others. To change one *from* one's own actual interior events only.

PART IV: CONVERTED FROM LANGUAGE

12. AMBER TURTLES

Translucent amber-hairs on bulb on tiny aged one who skitters humped crosses the walk in front of one.

A couple are sleeping together; beside them, a figure is zoomed up as: bouncing up *from* the darkness is being it. The woman beside him, whom he'd copulated (beneath him—he is trying to resuscitate her) chokes and dies as if squeezed into the other side (of night air)—*with* the jealous figure who'd leapt as that air, though who hasn't died yet herself, but has zoomed (is in two zones at once) sometimes remembered. By him, by anyone—but the figure is there (in *their* separate place, at night). (He'd had an affair with this other:) he gets help to secretly remove her corpse which carried, the moon huge white dilates the landscape which is heard insects in huge whiteness so it is *as*, thus in, night's darkness at once: where they carry the corpse, her long hair suddenly spills out dragging. He, young, weeps hysterically.

The whole society founded on selling the girls, the parents may sell a girl though they are not starving, are prosperous, for a television or video—yet the girls rebel still.

The limbs of one girl on her back struggle, as they attack her in a tiny room surrounding her. She's collapsed under only their brutal complete amber force always. Any number of them.

Eleven or twelve year olds, and girls who resemble these, receive a higher price. Many thousands return to towns dying of AIDS, where the girls are rejected and starve on the street. (The people in the towns dying also.) It's seen, but not modified being monetary.

Two persons efface, claim having made a movement, the members, who are grateful supplicants for being obliterated [chumps] in their movements [not] existing being only those two person's 'descriptions' *as* [their own past] accomplishments, *the past continually*—*no movements ever*. When they see that someone sees this, they destroy them. Yet are friends only when one is no longer duped. People call "brilliant" being actions of rip-off business market.

The forest wrecked is black soot gray ash and shiny with sweat, where the workers move like ghosts in and out of the smoke around the ovens,

Grace, when she'd stumbled in, had said to Cloe. Grace sank translucent into the tub, wedge-shaped basin, and floating in the hot water lies in her cubicle, apartments like stalls everywhere. Where one hears others around one urinating in the stalls next to one or moving in them—they bump the sides of their stalls. She feels comfortable and the soft form floats in the bath with no bottom of the basin touching her. The shallow basin is bottomless pool there (for her). The paint is chipped on the walls in the bathroom, she notices, not usually observing this.

The purple scars and bone, that are what the slaves become everywhere, their fat burned off of them from the heat from their feeding the charcoal ovens, are now purple-imprint burned on the inside of her closed eyelids, when they are closed. As she's lying in the bath.

She reads the imprints floating there in the basin. The imprint floats in the basin 'also.' Her flesh wavers in the water equally with the imprint (that's in her eyes). Her impression. Even weariness is equal faculty.

There is a bleed-through everywhere.

Cloe leaves, closing Grace's apartment door. Cloe's relieved. When Grace hadn't appeared anywhere, Cloe'd come to look for her. Though Grace had been canned, fired by Robespierre, Cloe a junior officer hadn't expected Grace to accept this. Grace hadn't.

The young woman Cloe enters the stream on the street, then. Pretty soon, a boy who'd lowered the kickstand of his motorbike and stepped into the people attracts her because he has a jack in the back of his head.

Seriality is objective, may be a way of repeating absurdity so it's objective. Cloe's a uniformed cop following the boy until he turns his front to her and walking backward in the crowd speaks to her playfully. The crowd is speaking playfully, so he is. She thinks. It's a crowd of boys only.

Let me buy you a sandwich, Cloe invites. The crowd ruffles and speaks playing, the boy has tufts of blond hair on his scalp unevenly, the spikes of the hair floating in the crowd. Esau de Light—someone else named me, for an event. She's asked his name. Walking.

A tiny humped aged lady, whose red hair thinned on her bulb which appears to come before the hump-the fused shoulders on the tiny mound passes skittering in front of them. Seen is (at its) the tiny amber-hump's side. Passes in front of Cloe.

Antonio returns to Grace's cubicle for a rest. Exhausted, he soaks in the tub, the porcelain basin of translucent nude man. Seen by the one in it, the outside, seems at once, so he lies stretched out sunk on the bottom.

Tiny aged lady has amber hair (so thin the hairs are as if antennae) translucence that's behind the hump skittering, when seen to the side. Having crossed the walk, the amber-haired hump is seen at the back.

Land. Why are there no women? asks Cloe lifting her leg onto the stool at a café. They're all in brothels, Esau de Light says simply. For the police (they're paid) return the girls who escape, and the girls are sometimes killed for rejecting being in the brothels, or beaten and made to be with fifteen men every night. There are millions sold impinging on the entire polis. Only a few vote. The system everywhere, there's no way to escape. Anyone else scoffs at this.

Cloe asks, Were there girls sold from your family also? He merely smiles, his lip drooping in a shrug as the smile that's in his eyes has that. The eyes reflect the shrug which can't exist in them. I have no family, he says as if she's dumb. But he's friendly.

They eat sugar and it sets off craving. Seated.

People are tactful when they want to accomplish something, they change it by speaking only. A bellicose man was being merely selfish one time, even when opposing. That man gets useless attention, in the sense that it does nothing to change outside. It's directed to *him*. Cloe laughs. They're walking on the street away from the café when a man puts his hand on Cloe's arm. He's detaining her though she's strong and pulls away wrestling with him.

Pimps are here. She's so beautiful it doesn't even matter to the pimp that she's in the police.

Cloe wrestles with the man. Esau de Light, the boy snatching her, is on his motorbike riding sideways in the light then that transfixes and crossing the layers of cubicles where the girls live and work in the illumined stalls that are visible from the side, is near their layers in air, motorbike spurting sideways on the street and is in the air above the street. Only the motorbike is there. Cloe and the boy fall from it in the air.

Making is useless. One woman doesn't appear to consider making a thing as if there were no difference, between there being something or not. Suffering is useless. The eyes beaten closed are felt (material). A girl who'd rebelled had been found with her neck cut, the police having sent her back, after she'd escaped and been caught.[1]

The forest goes by, its stumps (not in a middle swatch that can be seen, driving) swim unseen, what's in that middle path is visible. *A baseless realm—a realm of basis—is even with it.*

1. *Disposable People: New Slavery in the Global Economy*, Kevin Bales, University of California Press, Berkeley, 2000.

13. SEEING THE DEAD AND THEY DON'T KNOW THEY'RE DEAD

"They're everywhere"[1]—all the time—(as they're us)
Negative space placing outside and inside together
Seated across from her, her lips seep belligerence in fleshy mockery. Eyes squinting steely flesh-eyes seep contempt, a corrosive deliberate mockery of Grace. The unknown woman's eyes glint coals. She is laughing hatred of the one viewed—in that 'the-viewed' has a contemplative faculty (in *their being*, and in *they're being* interested in anything).

This view is also corrosive to the viewer, the one seeping contempt: the pugnacious bully, a bubble head bleached blonde turned to seed in fleshy hatred. Yet by the very fact of that, she has no sense of that ever (except anger towards others). Idle, even if working hard in office or service work, nothing that requires thought or concentration, because the nature is left fallow but never entered at all, she has nothing outside. Though she sits on material goods.

Grace is seated at the café waiting for Andrew. Grace glances then withdraws her eyes. The fleshy filled with contempt comes to the edge of it as if a deer. She's seated at the next table. Grace has to meet him in café Soft deer, thinks Grace. Really, she is (Grace thinks, of the other in front of her, who is jealous. *if Grace could alleviate it*). Though the other hates with all her violent power, huge. Having too much drink, eating, and empty stormy relations with people, which seem filled because they're stormy. Supine, a sensualist that is a kettle boiling her sensuality.

---

1. The film *The Sixth Sense*. A little boy can see the dead out with wounds in them. They want to speak to him as he has the ability (not 'skill') to see and hear them.

Even heavenly warbling of woman singing is closed to this sensual boil, though once she sang. She is an unknown, not seen by Grace before, or again. Materialist, Grace muses, considering the one there in front of her.

The boy sees the dead, who died in accidents, illness, murdered or died old walking everywhere intermingling at every instant with us (who haven't yet died). The sensualist of hatred can't see this, the dead continually beside us, that's why she hates, for one thing. Has contempt for any seeing, for physical sight (not realizing she's doing it, it's ordinary). She's a fly, bored, sips her wine. Mad because she doesn't want to do anything, though she may work like crazy. Poor.

Grace waiting in front of this other for Andrew, their office is wired to record all conversations, all is public, every individual in public is wired and receives monitoring. Bullhorns in the towns scream orders beginning at dawn. Waking order one. If one can hear that language. But the monasteries of the occupied-inferior have no bullhorns, still. A falcon flies beside one, broken people.

'We're' 'forced' to not use language—?—others merely appear as pod-flowers in that they don't 'see' (image. The word is "reality," then why not use "reality"—no, no, drive the reality out. Then there's only image) their 'self' or others.[2]

Another doesn't want to see herself or others, at all. Does not approach things in this way (what's occurring has no relevance)? 'Her not to see her, at all' isn't a change, it's what's been but one couldn't see this—it's a social custom also.

The social re-interpretation of one—as (any one/others) *being* the outside 'only' ('social' is all there is)—that very implosion is also 'akin' to (or is) one's *'inner life'*: until it is scrutiny, clear.

Here, to be outside of the outside, not to conform to the outside, is viewed as 'only' alienation-despair as if one were merely *not popular*. Then, there is no *public* at all *as* communal.

---

2. "No, no, drive the reality out." The film *King Lear* by Jean-Luc Godard.

As inner life there *isn't* public at all—'for that which is public' to occur is only *as* inner life (one and communal in the outside).

> "… the outside which is outside and the inside which is inside are not when they are inside and outside are not inside in short they are not existing, that is inside, and when the outside is entirely outside that is is not at all inside then it is not at all inside and so it is not existing."[3]

An occurrence itself is reinterpretation only:

> Social conception as 'how things are seen at the time' also predicates that there is no 'seeing occurrence' (any which is *not* formed by the social).
>
> 'Seeking in order to re-form the outside' by 'one being it only'—is seen (by the materialist) only as 'being the same thing as the outside' (seeking popularity-power-trash). One is there only as *oneself being space.*

'To see' (outside of) this can't be 'in' language. At all. Because that is oneself. *Because language is oneself only.*

> "To live in the glass house is a revolutionary virtue par excellence"[4] …Once the cozy *intérieur* is gone "another space opens up. It is violent, surreal, and bacchanalian space, where the political sphere and what was under cover…implode in a space"[5] …so that no member remains untorn."[6]

A Buddhist analogy to Walter Benjamin's glass house (living in a state of revolution)—is living as apprehension that is no allusion to anything, is not 'in' language (and [while aware] language is *only* allusion).

'apprehending occurrence'—as there *not being* language or creating exterior—*is* illusion/allusion. Impossible 'as itself within language.' This sense of the impossible *is* the opportunity of (is the event that is) 'apprehending occurrence.'

---

3. *Stein: Writings 1932*-1946, Gertrude Stein, The Library of America, 1998, page 346.

4. Walter Benjamin quoted in *Theater, Theory, Speculation: Walter Benjamin and the Scenes of Modernity,* Rainer Nägele, The Johns Hopkins University Press, Baltimore, Maryland, 1991, page 65.

5. Ibid., page 72, page 74.

6. Walter Benjamin quoted, Ibid., page 74.

And Andrew Chen's mother dying—split from her physically.

The dead are outside everywhere in the movie *The Sixth Sense* but they are everyone.

All are dependent, are formed by each other. The task of Tibetan *Secret Autobiographies* is to apprehend that state that is 'neither the outside nor inside creating the other'—bring about the instant of that in seeing. Which occurs at once, *when everything is dependent* ('when' there's no single phenomenon by itself).

That is (occurs) as exactly what it is, was—no image of it even. Drive the image out.

> Evening walking in the past, M mentions her mother. Earlier, when one was expressing fear, of the disks in the neck being removed and fused, M snarled *That is nothing! My mother had that. And it was nothing!* One having said then one was frightened, she who's a friend having focused continually on serving for men, had not noticed the one being in pain. Evening walking *then* (later) says her mother had had an iron bar put in the length of her back.
>
> This raises *later* and then whether there is anything. Definition of one from the outside begins then (simultaneous with physiological dis-function at that moment).
>
> Does M have no imagination. How is the iron bar in the back. Women are to be (are) servants so they should not be ill. "Rebelling" is a *non sequitur*, assuming there is any given anywhere.
>
> There isn't. Apparently. Even flesh isn't a given, as it is not what the person is (at all. Or as servant. Though as female function 'it' is flesh but divorced from the person). Is that why the fundamentalists or Puritans view it as not to be spoken, what happens to one's flesh is not to be mentioned by one in public. Only customary behavior is valued (is of value to others).

So there can't be kindness existing—isn't—where one is 'dependent'—on others (but that's what kindness *is*!)—or where dependent on the value that is given to *others*. This experience is different from and surpasses distrust. Social custom, never having been seen before, is seen for the first time: 'everyone is entirely separate from it.'

In that, to speak this to people who are causing and outside the occurrence cannot affect the occurrence (is merely exteriorized).

Their *only* attacking someone else. If one speaks interpreting (language is nothing, only conceptual), one's only reversed as arising from one's flawed base. To define oppressors as "cruel" is *nothing*. Described as in the past a "feudal system," justifies the occupied being beaten now, imprisoned, their inner practice persecuted, their children taught a foreign language, fleeced of their resources which are consumed by their imperialist occupiers—*place most indicative of the modern world*

but silence internalizes and imprisons—if that is one's inner life also

if one speaks that will alleviate—*it cannot change what occurs. as language.*

but also outside. *changes outside.*

that they were feudal is a *non sequitur as language.* (unrelated

that one had anger, or love, or had illness the body dying— is a *non sequitur* in their imposition) as *one's* is not that which *is* their 'outside.' their imposition. which is any *one* is nothing.

heavenly warbling of woman singing is not heard by a woman who earlier did sing

It is 'social': 'to think the body is nothing'—*puritanical is materialistic at once*

yet they're regarding 'conceptual' as imposition only, *also*

mock one's conceptual speaking as if their patriarchy were not anti-conceptual (forbidding seeing its construction) and *that* repression and defining is regarded as good!

Intellect (language) is related to outside events *as* (it is) one's inner life (one makes this relation)—so it perishes 'only.' That one separates 'people' at all from 'what occurs' outside even—is also one's inner life (then not enabling one to see *them*).

Everything 'continually'—it seems to be continuous.

'Evening walking' isn't continuous though—it's 'evening walking'

(It's continuous.) Or it's 'raining flowers evening.'

suffering is easiest to *be* in language. weighs. convert it. in 'evening walking'

T is amused and mysterious. separately. *continuous alleviates.*

with him. one. is in heaven. that is one's inner life. their. with others and 'evening walking'

one 'has to' be 'converted from language'—'has to' not exist as it—at once—in the present also the past. no that's not spatial running forward. not—to rush forward—*as joy spatial-crowd-only*

and that exists 'as' one's inner life also

Bright Dark, Pal Mal Comic

The mines are dangerous. Miners are crushed. Roses on the walls.

Work in grueling labor, and injured, ill with black lungs are discarded. There is no insurance. Union representatives are murdered, anyone trying to start a union even. Antonio claims injury, that he can't speak at all. He's waiting to collect. Had to pass their doctor's inspection (the miner's doctor, risking, agrees with Antonio's description of injury—so they kill that doctor, who's found)—their company doctors examine him. Though the company has said it will pay, they will wait for any mistake (in which he speaks inadvertently, because he's trying to undermine them) will find out he can speak and kill him.

His claim is his larynx removed by the doctor who's dead or he's been scared after a mine accident he can't speak—he'd have to be entirely silent. To pass.

Dark hair, his eyes dark, purses his lips to smile, in that he has to restrain noise, restrain joking or laughing, any slip of sound from his larynx, who'd gnashed his teeth glinting holding his brother's corpse to his chest. Where he's impassioned, angered by the company killings. He's removed his shirt, changing.

Bare-chested, he exchanges a look in the room with Grace who aware that the fraudulent claim may get him killed cooperates but forgets and asks him questions (she forgets and speaks as if he would answer) about eating or details, asides spoken to him. Her apartment bugged, they wear wires like everyone—he makes no sound though. Seeing him shirtless—he turns on the radio loudly then. He puts a stick in his mouth, a bit like a horse.

The chest, taking her in his arms—and for the first time undressing her, removes the bra, only her facial expression (that he has to go against the company, but she thinks his claim, that's angry revolt trying to outfox them, may fail) remains (between them) he's lying on her the part with his back arched is in her and thrashing flat then on her, the bit is between his teeth comes, only when she already has.

Where lying on her slow flat his length on her that's also the length of the part up in her, his muscular flesh and considerate waiting, slowing, holding the bit in his teeth which causes him to come, he's waited cupping her head with his hands while still lying his full length on her—him not yet coming. But her legs closed so that he's lying on his part up in her between her closed legs, they come both. The bit in the mouth restraining his grunting even, yet riding on her gently cupping yet the part coming out puts it in again slowly, on her, then comes after he's waited for her to.

The radio is playing loudly, speakers, yet he senses by feel the place that she'll be.

The wind is outside cracking something against the building. When he's lying with his full length on her and then arched his back, comes he puts his mouth up to the side of her ear but the bit is still between his teeth restraining him from speaking. Or noise. A place that's a grid also. When the part is full length in her and moving on that in her legs held on it he doesn't grunt even or make any sound, his eyes bursting bright dark.

They're inside a container, but not in their flesh, their flesh is outside.

Our soldiers see one of our soldiers fall from the helicopter and see he's caught by enemy soldiers underneath as the helicopter wallows in the air. Theirs catch him underneath. He's found slain later, left behind.

But there's a balance. Feeling the place that she'll be, before coming to it, that he does and with his mouth with the bit in it at her ear as he's plunging, still as if to murmur in her ear, his eyes do that.

She just comes up to his eyes, her hands gripping the flesh on his back.

14. TREASURE DISCOVERER

In Tibetan *Secret Autobiography*, visionary experience and treasure discovery are linked. Texts hidden in one generation are later envisioned and found. The discovery is the basis of the Treasure discoverer making a claim to legitimization of their personal identity—that is, that they *are* that previous individual who hid the text (these are called "Earth Treasures"). This visionary practice:

> "assumes the truth of reincarnation, but it goes further than most Asian traditions, and even further than other institutions of Tibetan Buddhism, which are already exceptional for their system of recognizing and enthroning children as reincarnations of deceased masters. Yet the notion that someone could have been appointed in a past life to discover a hidden text in this life was widely accepted in the milieu in which Jigme Lingpa was raised... When he went into retreat, the meditations he performed were based on famous Treasure cycles. This immersion helped set the stage for Jigme Lingpa's own Treasure revelation and begins to explain why he considered such an experience to be at the heart of his identity."[1]

Janet Gyatso, in the passage that follows, applying a western materialist critique interprets Treasure tradition 'anthropologically' in terms of the subject's careerism, rather than 'from within,' in the terms of their own culture. Jigme Lingpa sees certain figures in his visions, which *are* revelatory of reality; therefore evidence of *his* accuracy. Gyatso views their vision as

---

1. *Apparitions of the Self: The Secret Autobiographies of a Tibetan Visionary*, Janet Gyatso, Princeton University Press, Princeton, New Jersey, 1998, page 145.

careerism, rather than the practice that's discovery; this peels them apart from their intention:

"The Treasure tradition served as a vehicle for religious figures to distinguish themselves outside of the conventional monastic and academic avenues for self-advancement. The specificity of time and personal identity that goes along with being a Treasure discoverer confers uniqueness and individuality, and…the Treasure discoverers are among the most prolific writers of autobiography in Tibetan literary history… The other main kind of Treasures are the 'Mental Treasures' (dgongs-gter), which are said to have been hidden in the discoverer's memory; these are accessed in visionary experience… Somewhat less subject to suspicion than the Earth Treasures, the Mental Treasures are affiliated with the larger 'Pure Vision' (dag-snang) tradition of India and Tibet, in which meditators have visions of deities who preach sacred teachings. Pure visions, however, lack the kind of historical assertions that are made in the Treasures."[2]

Conceptual is physiological (historical assertion). Also, one jumping generations to be someone else is outside of one's physiological-conception (at any time). *Secret Autobiography* is the present in one's own life-time (it's different from discovering Earth Treasures, is coincident with Mental Treasures).

Perhaps Janet Gyatso, in that passage, is 'translating' for (into) American culture: there's a distinction between phenomena being non-translatable (being only as a culture or individual, can't exist other than that) and 'only not-translated is it.'

Deer Night (a poem-play/'account' I wrote) is a form of *Secret Autobiography*, sparked by events in 1996—in particular, a crowd (in Bhutan) of mocking Westerners impinging into the Bardo dance which was underway (during which I was perched standing on a rung of a cliff with children, viewing the scene vertically), onlookers entering to bow to the incoming figure of death.

Deer Night is intended to be read silently and also to be enacted (and to be the experience of these going on in one

---

2. Ibid., pages 146-147.

simultaneously and separate as reading on the retina). *Seeing* the crowd in 1996 in Bhutan enacted a particular spatial-mental gyration: which had occurred in me when I was fourteen. *Seeing* is in itself outside.

As: All Occurrence in Structure, Unseen—Deer Night (using example of my own text in *The Public World/Syntactically Impermanence*)[3] is:

Text as physiological-conceptual tracking of—that is—reoccurrence. It is a particular schism/gyration of 'the inside of the inside' *being* 'the outside of the outside' (at once).

> It is not that others would be interested in a feeling or early experience of mine, someone they don't know anyway. Rather, I'm trying to find there being any real-time instant at all. In anyone. If I try to see it, it isn't real, and *now* it's romanticism. The present then was not then romanticism.

Deer Night is syntax of split or shape, a schism/gyration (of an earlier event—which was: 'getting it' that there's death—*experienced* by me as a kid at age fourteen; it has a particular past). The syntax is that early spatial shape (as at age fourteen), but the interior-exterior shape occurring in 1996. The source no longer exists (as event or emotion—neither response to the earlier split nor to the later event of the dance). The early event (at fourteen) in which a split occurred is not separable from the later spatial-syntax-gyration (the text). The text is reoccurrence of that particular earlier conceptual (spatial) configuration but in *Deer Night* it is syntax, *not* transcriptions of events as content of that early time (rather, events as 'interiorized' then, not 'known'). This is for one the inside of the outside. Seeing history outside 'that person' (one), *in* oneself—later, in a crowd.

Forgotten mental tracks manifested in me then (at age fourteen) as a spatial-interior-gyration without language—which are now translated (sparked by seeing the crowd without language) as a spatial-syntax-gyration: that *is* the experience (the text). The two interiors-and-syntax (two) which *are* a schism *is* the experience.

---

3. *The Public World/Syntactically Impermanence*, Leslie Scalapino, Wesleyan University Press, Middletown, Connecticut, 1999.

Rendering the experience (of three times) in *Deer Night* can't occur if one only describes the events that produced the writing. It is outside one, inside one? What's an event *or* a memory (separate)? So the event has no existence.

(To try to describe again:) The text's syntax is 'the same as' that earlier shape that occurred in one. It's a spatial motion, not a 'memory' (content). No event as that is reproduced or articulated. No one else can be that exactly.

The spatial motion of this split (as: 'the inside of the inside' *being* 'the outside of the outside') was merely *learned* in (as) the prior occurrence, as dancers learn motions and conceive as and reproduce those motions.

The motions are a 'relation' only. One sees in 'it' one is constructed only, memory is only implanted. One did not theorize it, theorizes it later; but the two (experiencing and theorizing it) *are* oneself (and the event). Early then, the U.S./world/ oneself had been (was then) imperialism military conceptual transforming the off-world colonies, which was also 'one' constructed only (aware of that of, *then* early, theorizing anyone dying, at all. The first time of theorizing that. That we do, have to). "I'm not *in* the business. I *am* the business."

Thus the reader is both 'other' and 'oneself' throughout.

The text as 'reading' that is itself 'configuration-tracking' is in the nature of Tibetan 'historical assertions.' The early (and later) configurations were 'actual' as 'physiological-conceptual' rather than being psychology or events.

Analytical is the same as a motion.

The skateboarder has the skill of diving and looping in the L.A. aqueducts. It isn't translated, conceptual is it.

In so far as *Deer Night* is an *entire* re-writing of Shakespeare's *Tempest* (without any of his characters, plot, or language)—(his was the imperial world, the beginning of England's imperialism)—is placing a gesture into it: being is total imperialism 'of' oneself. Which spatial motion reoccurring—exposes it, but then it simply reoccurs in one some other time, a rupture in *that* time. There isn't any *other* self?

It is 'the place of that which is prior.' Or, before it occurs.

Which is at the same time: everyone is colonized, all peoples all individuals are in colonies—*as* any mind (itself being social-physiological layers of events (colonization), which like a flower, its petals-layers motion are also theory only) *is* that which is 'existing' at all:

> "The mind: not as the characteristic of fragile or the characteristic of being out in experience only—but being experience only.
>
> which is one's motions."[4]

These motions (in the text) *are only experience*. Also, the analytical *is* that only.

There are 'two sides' (fabrication of boundary) which cannot be translated into each other, and *are* the inverse/converse/introversion of other as such. And that converse is experience separate from, by only being, its analytical side. This is physical motion there.

(Wrestling in one [at the time, now] *is* that split.)

'Intellectual construct' (idea only, not in its sound or shape) is imitation of being, yet representation as the 'theory'—as if that's the figure's shell (seen from outside, or in DNA) rather than its motion?

My interpretation of Nāgārjuna's thought (he was Indian, pre-Christ Zen thinker) is juxtaposed in *Deer Night* as demonstration. His thought is not a model: I'm not 'writing Nāgārjuna' which would be then only to have *his* authority; but rather, the intent is to divest *any* authority, one's own or any other. An 'outside-logic' is a cue.

My interpretation of Nāgārjuna's logic:

a present-time self, a place, or occurrence is not the same as its historical/physiological (prior) instance. One *there* even (*then*) (as duplication or as memory) is not the same as the earlier occurrence. (So there is no 'earlier occurrence' of 'anything.')

---

4. Ibid., page 97.

A present-time self isn't *not* its instance *then* either. Nor is it the same thing as only 'itself' *now* (as if no relation to its earlier occurrence).

A present instance or self isn't 'arising' from an earlier beginning either (if it's 'now'). This means everything is 'impinged on' completely and so doesn't occur as 'impingement' even. Impinged on 'completely,' one knows oneself only as the 'present moment.' Which can't even exist.

There's a surface comparison of Nietzsche's view to Nāgārjuna's, as described by James Porter in *The Invention of Dionysus: An Essay on the Birth of Tragedy* (p. 8): "Nietzsche could affirm in 1866 that our inner and outer sensations alike are the 'products of our organization' and that the concept of a thing in itself, divorced from its conceptual support in this organization (which is also its source), threatens to plummet into pure meaninglessness." There's a difference between nihilism/meaninglessness and Nāgārjuna's relativity (which holds no such interpretation).

Nāgārjuna's view is that opposites are maintained, not resolved—to the extent that they can't even *exist* as *opposites* (since even opposition/rupture is 'holding to a view,' is existing).

Nāgārjuna's radical opposition to cause and effect is similar to Benjamin's view of tragedy quoted in Rainer Nägele's *Theater, Theory, Speculation: Walter Benjamin and the Scenes of Modernity*. Nägele quotes Benjamin:

> "It is in the nature of epic theater that the undialectical opposition of form and content of consciousness (which leads to the situation where dramatic figures can relate to their actions only in reflections) is replaced by a dialectical relation of theory and praxis (that leads to the situation where the action opens up, at the points of its ruptures, to a view of theory).
>
> "In its continuous mirroring of the always already given phenomena and images, reflection remains caught in the prison of the imaginary. Only where the symbolic, the inexpressive, 'the commanding word,' and writing (*Schrift*) violently and inexorably interfere, is the magic spell of the imaginary broken.

> "The imaginary is essentially linked with the image of the body; its phantasmatic investment is in the integrity and wholeness of the body as *Gestalt* and indivisible."[5]

This can't be 'known' in order to occur. It is rupture. One takes apart the image of the body. Has to in that it is introverted also.

> "The black butterfly on black night is introverted, as his supposed inferior nature is.
> so the liquid black (night) isn't a past—one
> in resting in it has no present/future. (And as seen by us.)
> (Not being a future by itself, it can only be a present/future.)"[6]

Social qualities ("The black butterfly on black night is introverted")—the entire there is only social, and *'neither'* (black butterfly or black night) 'is' social. Nor is there any *'neither'*—the spaces displace themselves.

Relation to: writing that is outside what the mind can do. Not simply what *that* mind can do. At all. There. It is 'something else' than one's own mind. Writing is reading at once.

'Theorizing oneself' as body that is conceptual (such as seeing within the body, not on the eye's retina, which is the intention of the text in *Deer Night*)—is reversing the imaginary. Imitating the 'body's conceptualization' (there is no wholeness, only conceptual) *is* disruption.

In (the text of which *Deer Night* is a past) *The Public World/ Syntactically Impermanence*, the essays are placed first *in order*

---

5. *Theater, Theory, Speculation: Walter Benjamin and the Scenes of Modernity*, Rainer Nägele, The Johns Hopkins University Press, Baltimore, Maryland, 1991, pages 161-162.

6. *The Public World/Syntactically Impermanence*, Leslie Scalapino, Wesleyan University Press, Middletown, Connecticut, 1999, page 117.

there to change the whole structure—by placement.[7] 'Analytical' is rupture, taking 'subject' out of itself. Therefore to have 'analytical' be *'before,'* to precede—'is exterior events only' (referring to mass events, wars, crowds, sights). The relation (of the division between that and interiority, by theory being placed before motion-occurrence) is:—exterior/theory is the *same* as those motions, *as* the converse, *there*. The division wipes away the division. Dismantle history.

The spatial occurrence had to actually be and I had to derive (theorize) it prior to other theory impacting it (it *is* its theory)—that is, I didn't know it; I didn't think of it afterwards; it *is* historical occurrence (in *Deer Night*, in myself as a kid at fourteen) in order for one to be. Thus one isn't?

It has to be *'only in oneself' which is theorized*—in order for (there to be) 'not dying' or 'not defined utterly' social *and* phenomena.

A corollary: it is 'specific as my identity only' *as* outside of my identity.

The Replicants (like Tibetan Khampas[8]), robotic *imitation*

---

7. Ibid. I'm speaking here about my intention (in *The Public World/Syntactically Impermanence*) in placing the essays before the poetry: there is a separation so that neither is introduction to the other, or afterword (separation as chrysalis and butterfly), yet the intention was to transform across both sides of the barrier.

8. Khampa horsemen, Tibetan tribal "cowboys" who in guerilla warfare fought the Chinese invaders: "protected by their knowledge of the wild, high-altitude terrain, wrought widespread destruction on the enemy's lifeline, ambushing supply columns and raiding military posts,...cutting communications, seizing territory with ferocious bravura" (*Tears of Blood: A Cry for Tibet*, Mary Craig, Counterpoint, Washington, D.C., 1999, pages 71-72). They used rifles, daggers, and swords against armoured cars, tanks, automatic machine guns, and military aircraft, later fought by riding in from high-altitude Himalayan Lo Monthang, Mustang, a Buddhist enclave in Nepal. In response to Khampa resistance (this part of Tibet was subsequently subsumed as a Chinese province, said no longer to be part of Tibet-proper) entire villages were wiped out, with hundreds of public executions to intimidate the survivors, nuns and monks forced to copulate in public, many sent to death camps.

"more human than human," in the film *Blade Runner*, have implants of memories.

Just as the Treasure discoverers are searching for clues that track their former incarnations (the Treasures having been hidden in a former life, one demonstrates specificity of ones by verification of that life, being its future), the Replicants keep treasures such as photos which document their memories—implants from outside.

However, the Replicants' implants are created by the biogenetic engineering wizard, Tyrell. In that the Replicants have only a short-time to store up experience, implanted memories are intended by Tyrell to serve as an emotional cushion for them whereby the Replicants can be more easily controlled as slaves to humans in off-world colonies. In that they have attachments, they go on to create their own emotions and experiences: so can be conceptually enslaved by memories, is Tyrell's intention.

The Replicant, Roy, says: "Quite an experience to live in fear, isn't it? That's what it is to be a slave."

'The sensitive intricate as being perception Rachel' who learns that she is a Replicant, did not know.

There *was* no difference between her and humans except for *her* to know 'later' that she is constructed. "I am not *in* the business. I *am* the business."

A psyche-split occurs, she flees, and will have to be "retired" (execution). Humans use 'poor' words, inadequate and far less eloquent imagined in experience than those not-human.

Those not-human create their own emotions and experiences—while being politically and physiologically enslaved: laboring, and also enslaved in brothels; hunted and "retired" if they escape; also programmed to die as four-year life scheme. They've come to the first world to reverse their conceptual structure, to stop the death process.

They create their own emotions and experiences as "humans" which is both 'theorized' (in that they see themselves as machines) and 'in experience.' Thus they are "more than human."

The conceptual structure is irreversible, physiological (the built-in four-year life span).

His "moments" occurred 'outside' of memories as implants (they are *not* implants but creations *as* these). They are in their real past and future at once. Yet the off-world—the colonies are the vast unseen, of which there are no flashbacks or forward— is the enslaved present then.

It is a military present. Oneself (as being 'theorizing,' and 'experience' as that) can only 'be' by escaping off-world colonies and world, that is, by actual action. Now. Inside the relation, or being the relation only, that is between conceptual and world.

Deer Night written is read by the isolated reader in silence also 'action' as if a play but that is on the retina of one (reading the outside)—pressure 'that moment of reading is there can't be action (at all)—the past and present being gone—and there's *only* that also.'

Anxious that one can't act, anyone—there's no action in any present-time moment—in life—is seeing living then. Even actions and events *seen* can't be.

And this is only conflict—of one, the isolated reader—so that 'the outside' (also that interiorized as oneself) scrutinizes 'conflict-as-one' as not being uniform, the crowd. Yet is the individual-as-crowd. That it *not* be individual, single, is conflict there while it is seen with individual features.

A text that is outside the limitations of language (intrinsic conflict):

To write a text that is sight, without sound even—as if it could be only the sight of events. And thus has no conflict. Yet language inherently is *not* silence; even if language is not spoken aloud, it is sound in one.

Have 'written' be *only the sight of events*, only physiological seeing—the instant when 'that sight of an event occurs only *when* it is the written.'

Yet one could rest while in proximity 'with' real occurrence? Rest is seeing only.

A text could be able to see events outside of sequencing. But our 'ordinary' seeing (eyes 'physiological'—and meaning also: 'conventional' view, which is social) *also* 'sequences.'

Seeing that is free of sequencing is akin to Tibetan Treasure Discovery which is historical assertion (someone or something that actually occurred): 'written which is only physically seeing events' is to form from the 'reverse side' of historical events. Events one has not *seen*, can't physically be seen even can be rendered

Dream RT (in the dream having read this writing, "4. Treasure Discoverer") indicates it 'didn't do it,' isn't anything—saying it's just trying to show I'm tough, how tough I am. I ask him what should I do? I should just throw it away? He says no, I should do it really 'as interiorly.' The implication is I'd have to rewrite *Deer Night* utterly ('interiorly') which in present would be—'it, as if the same entity exactly, *in utter happiness.*'

Traveling on a golden plain. In real-time, in Mongolia gold plain and indigo sky. They are the inside because I wrote them— are not spoken, nor are they 'the places themselves.'

Flower, Pal Mal Comic Book

The daisy-cutter has wasted some, thinks Cloe O'Brien almost flinching as she peers at a shredded liquid ball on which a face had emerged and still floats briefly. Say how.

Except Cloe is very young. Her long slender limbs move in the street in the wind still blowing from the whirling daisy-cutter (weapon). Reading is unseen, is below and calm.

Realistic. 'Picture this' is the same as acceptance of it— passivity—in that here they are flowers that are duplications of themselves as physical appearance but without their original. Without any original. Or any being.

An old friend saying "We have to be realistic," the occurrence of war and acceptance of it are the same ('realistic' *then*). The citizens are individuals physically—but they are uniform with each other? If one remarks their consuming and killing, he calls one elitist, as if uniformity were a way of looking at things that is central.

Everywhere, the ones outside, who are not us, are simply entirely other than us. One is not allowed to speak of them even—or one is elitist—Who's, the white media man says, seeing is "privileged voyeurism of other cultures." One's sight is polluted—so, one who is here is sufficiently cut off from oneself

while the Taliban (those with whom we are at war, they're outside us) decrees people shall not look at images or read.

Not oneself—in comic book strips—the writing is automated.

Cloe O'Brien looks. At a pod-flower ripped open by a daisy-cutter (weapon). We do not see anyone torn open here, for a while. Later we do. In ocean born may come up, may surface.

While there is no social recourse, social is only force. Of others.

Its tentative features are still lingering. The interior is still duplicating the features of some person. Uh, Cloe thinks or observes without speaking, looking at it.

The old friend says that those who critique should not, as critique will be seen as negative. Duh. The postcolonialist Saïd should not critique the west (the man says), as this can't be heard (by us). Have to hear what we accept.

Another man says You shouldn't put this in here because it's an argument

She says critique has to be heard, to change. While the man's supporting bombing Afghanistan—she's not doing so—he says You are only a privileged daughter and wife, voyeur—nothing in, or that is, one—while

the Afghani women wear robes from head to toe and are not allowed to go to school. He means that woman here not so constrained, is nothing and is elitist at the same time.

Lying beside a recomposing flower is a small *boy* then. Hurt, he has a gash in his midsection. So, another boy runs by. It doesn't follow.

We'd have to take this apart on the most minute level, all the time.

PART V: THE WEDGE

15. CLOE'S TURTLE

Cloe's amused, kicking garbage from her ankles, wading in it. Running. After falling from the motorbike, her sides are bruised and panting. The sides pant held still.

The girls are sold to brothels with no escape, beaten, raped cave in—or rebel until their deaths. The police collaborate to profit.

A lynx, her eyes large. Even running, she's amused that Esau de Light was named by someone else, named *for* someone else's *event*, something they saw before him? It commemorates.

They did something. She laughs. Her sides bleeding.

She's scraped on her arms and legs and on the side where her clothes are torn away, the skin shining, from her skimming on the street-side of the glancing bike—her seeing Esau de Light parting from his bike in the air.

Robed women are being beaten to one side on the street. Our military cements over the desert. It kills everyone by dropping daisy-cutters which shred them, and sets up hot-dog stands.

Drill oil there, shooting from holes in the cement. The military (separate from us) siphon their people's resources, control the people, beat them, and put in power those who beat them before.

Then it's no longer seen.

There isn't a relation to our war and those who put the girls in brothels and enforce their slavery—there isn't a relation

it'll keep introducing until the two, that which was introduced and that which is there before go on

People have tried that, not returning, that the content doesn't come back, is brief. This is just 'that it goes.' Go on

Cloe is not cynical at all, amused because she's young, is bruised everywhere and a big turtle comes up bursting the light at a market

it comes up breaking the surface and then comes at the sides, of a big tank made out of glass that's in public

a holding tank for people's amusement. It's butting looking out

it's an amber turtle with large eyes. The people are all small here. They imprison and beat everyone

the turtle butts the tank, looks out. The market bustles.

Cloe breaks the glass, and takes the turtle home. People come running but she's a policewoman, she's wearing a uniform

it's under arrest, she says, hustling it away. But it walks slow

she names it Hazel while it's walking

it swam up to the one spot where she could find it.

16. CONVERTED FROM LANGUAGE

They want to speak to him as he has the ability (not 'skill') to see and hear them.

The jacks in the boys who are not of human lineage have caused some kind of change—in them.

In the high altitude breathing from the bag only, the attachment which is carried in the day at day is separate from the dream of Mars. The dream is an unrelated event later, but which informs the other.

Flesh after suffering shock to it isn't linked later. The instant of their separate beings—is feeling itself?

Antonio is driving on the Richmond San Rafael Bridge, on the dazzling bay with flat tanker ships anchored beside the bridge's base. The bridge is a sway-back curve in the blue air on water at once. A woman is curled riding a motorcycle racing still in space to another woman, who curled on an other cycle far in front of them

The curled woman waits *for her* the other crouched hurling in space. At that instant Antonio stops breathing.

Asphyxiating, he's imploding inside. In the floating car his chest is still, the breath is not going in or out. He gets desperate then. There's a long time on the bridge. But his thorax is still still, it's isolated immovable hurling through the space of the span. On it.

The women curled crouch on the cycles far away from each other appearing to near each together as one is racing seeming still in the space in front of him.

Seeing that sight (his chest can't see—yet—and freezes)—that one is waiting for the other—seeing them in space at all (both? paralyze his thorax), he crazily laughs and weeping in the same time the thorax begins to breathe. To gulp air. His thorax sucks the air on the huge blue horizontal sheet.

Then he gets it that this is related to his brother's death, which had not been a thought in him while driving, as if it hadn't occurred. Hasn't this on the span—until he laughs and weeps at the same time.

The space—or those waiting in space (for each other?)—or *not* moving the one is curled fast lessening the space *in space*— seems to precipitate? this a separate person not breathing at all. So they, that person crazily laughing and weeping breathes.

In this space (event?), there's no place to dream, or space—

The woman curled in space, so her thorax is beside, almost submerged on cycle's thorax as the line of cycle and sky (as strung on bead)

not its speed,—yet the cycle (the curled woman on it) doesn't hurl while being out there—for the one driving behind it—the span of the bridge is so high in blue, everywhere there are no people

it's shot back in the center—spring, say. which doesn't move as them. and from very far away, on the other end—another woman waits lightly

flown ahead, one (behind) seeing it is seeing before—so that one can't breathe?

From far away on the thorax of her cycle, the woman's pressed jackknifed—the thighs don't curl in space

—then one (someone else) laughs and weeps in the same time (*in* it) so breathes.

Air Pal Mal (the frame)

A woman here saying pleasure is liberating, pain is *only* depersonalizing. is removing ego from one who is not having but is amidst them who *are* having pleasure? Or, the reverse of the same barrier in its instant—her gesture is to remove ego from *them* who *are* suffering? Oar.

The instant of their separate beings—is feeling itself?

A man here from his window sees people jump from

the high windows of the towers, crumbling beside him in the air, as they're crashed by the hijacked planes. Says he would like to see

people here advocate crushing bombing the Taliban that way

(they who are not the terrorists in the planes—not the same—nor are the people there).

expansion of (no) justice. Nothing to change him breaks into his saying this, whatever is said by others alongside him later—his speech still doesn't change. *He has to take it.*

Grace sits alone outside at a café. M and another, the-man-who-wants-faceless-motherslaves (P), are encountered in public after so long. They come up and seat themselves at a nearby table, with them a dowdy young woman who's soaking the sunken-flowered man with sympathy. The city is a savanna.

Evening is beginning and then the savanna is gold swaying. P suckles, but vicious, the conventions of moth-erhood so dead that it is only a slave. Sympathy is a type of flattery (that's to be *of him*).

He has no curiosity. Grace thinks.

The dowdy young woman has no friends, and no tal-ent! she says to herself seated outside. Then, recognizing that this is true she is ashamed of her own cruelty in noting this.

In the U.S., there appears to be only *actions* that are outside. Yet one(/the inside) isn't mechanistic. Or, interior change isn't.

One(/as inside) can't *be* those outside motions at all. Terror arises in one then that 'there are no actions in the present moment or ever' (even while these occur).

The savanna moves. Through the gold grass move oth-ers. Some at tables, a purse slung on a chair. A roar of overpass traffic fills the space.

P in aging, surrounds himself with flattery, accepts it from the lonely starved for affection, who, led by him, gratefully trashes others. As does M. No mercy appears in them. They trash Grace also, who sits 'by herself,' their teeth part as she listens.

Head turned away. In the stillness. In the past, friends—they'd taken her apart for having anger. May be she's unacceptable when speaking (speaking), which they can't recognize; would accept in a man. Or, looked down upon for concentrating on being in present time.

Whereas for them, the present is trivial. Not lush hierarchy. Led?—though they react to him not being flattered enough. sensation. they want lies. as if that were tradition.

a babyish image of a hyenadon, *our leader*, isn't custom, it is canned *as motions*

that are killing others. never pictured. (yet evening is not either pleasure or pain—*evening is pleasure*). as far as *M* is concerned, is evening trivial? (present. she's not a materialist)

Is thinking the present? Sometimes? It's slow and minute.

Grace doesn't harbor the gold savanna. (an action.) the evening so still is in the gold savanna.

The evening doesn't harbor the gold savanna also—feeling hurt bound by elegant M and the-man-who-wants-faceless-motherslaves isn't *in evening* (an emotion is *after* its origin, only, but *there* is no time except 'its' [possession]—evening is in the motion?)

M who criticizing blighting the inner nature of another (one after another) who're then inside-out and coming to her pleading with her *to speak* with *to come to meet* them then, she turns a cold shoulder to them, leaving them holding that pain themselves in prison which she reproduces ones—sitting outside, Grace begins to sing to try to locate Richard-the-Lion-Hearted in prison, he'll hear the song—but M butts in (she wants 'conceptual'/*interior*-status) snarling (when Grace had blurted fear—when our leader began bombing the innocent populace whom he will conquer, on the pretext that that is defense against a terrorist act here)

Innocent! M says Doesn't it make you want to weep for the innocent people (jumping from the towers and crushed killed) *here!* Forces weeping. Is she maintaining hierarchy and no time as it?

A spring. They changed the laws to allow unchecked infinite clandestine war. open. quash speaking here. compared (our hyenadon-leader/man-who-wants-faceless-motherslaves/evening/others) silent on 'either' side(s)—they do not crack or burst the repetition. or mirror. crack that inured. one. they're. outside.

alleviate.

without placating anyone, the scene—the leader *placed on the same space as* the ordinary man-who-wants-faceless-motherslaves ours banding with their former warlords holds their people in helpless poverty while ours fleece them—separate from the city that is a savanna waving touching one evening. the evenings are hardly separate. or *not* separate.

PART VI: WILD ICE

17. WILD ICE

A dream that refers to a real-time event: After a second spine operation, I dreamed traveling through an urban Mars embroiled cityscape moving in it, going toward where I was to have the operation again. Waking, I realized the dream was real-time memory of being operated upon from above while I'm inside my body (though dreaming, it's only translated as traveling). I'd been awake during it (though under general anesthetic). We're always awake. Here I refer to the event *and* the dream—the dream repeats the physical interior experience of the event, which is *its* occurrence both also.

This simultaneity occurs in the separation of the storyteller's speaking and the listening of those present.

The relation of character to action is horizontal on the waving, high, white grass. Is that different from seeing events silently? 'Silently' they're in real-time. Character is silent in relation to action, motion? Action is silent, is up close, and separates from the occurrence.

An eye held open unblinking all the time throughout—is the space. Earlier. Repetition:

The fall of the first boy, estimated by Jack Yeh (the coroner), would have to have been from a higher height than that of the building which bordered the alley where his corpse was found. He'd been moved. He'd ingested cocaine, had cocaine on his clothing.

Shoved and then moved from the same alley where, later, the second unidentified boy jumped? He's about fourteen years old (the second one, thinks Grace, irritated by her mind getting ahead to force an association of the two boys).

Hearing clattering inside in the kitchen, Cloe had squatted on the crumpled small corpse. The one who'd been moved after he fell.

About eleven or twelve years old, she estimated him.

Mostly Chinese immigrants there. Or Hispanic. He was found by a busboy who works at the restaurant, who'd been out having a smoke in the alley. Near the garbage cans, Cloe notices the remnants of a homeless person's bedding. Someone else, an adult probably, Cloe thinks.

She takes days of walking, the area filled with homeless who are living in the alleys and, at night or even day, on stoops of corporate or government buildings. She's trying to find the witness. They have their dogs with them as Cloe strolls Van Ness, four-lane lines of cars streaming, and turns off of Van Ness into the alleys.

Seated in the suite (of TORRID, a dot.com company), Grace interviews the janitress who describes the unfolding of events, starting with seeing the boy (who's later lying in the alley below) in the building before he'd fallen.

Dirk having removed Grace from her job—she's come to work anyway. Captain Jasper Frank dove-lids clucks his jowls a bit, calling Dirk again to clear it with him who never answers his calls. But Jasper Frank doesn't ask her to leave, or say anything to her. Not now, he ponders (though he may be suspended).

You entered the office, then he jumped from the window. Was the window open when you entered the room? Yes, her brows knit. Disturbed from remembering or from speaking, the woman kneeling seated small collected on the sofa.

Interviewed, the security guards of the building had seen nothing. Apparently, the boy had no means of entry, was admitted by someone else?

Cloe strolling,[1] she interviews homeless on Mission Street (the Hispanic neighborhoods of San Francisco). She asks first with one picture, then both. A boy darts away from her when

---

1. Long slender legs draped on a café bar stool, Cloe O'Brien drinks cappuccino leaning forward reading "Colombia Arrests 3 as I.R.A. Bomb Experts: Officials say Irish suspects aided Colombian rebels," an article in the *New York Times*.

she asks if he can identify the boys in the pictures. He sees the corpses in the photos and his face changes. Hey, she calls and runs after him but he disappears into a construction site.

The newspaper is as much as we will know of the two fallen angels, Grace had commented coming in. Boys fallen from the window. She had placed her purse on the desk.

The Feds have taken over the case and we are excluded while they're cooperating with our visitor from Colombia, Antonio, Grace continues. Cloe and Officer Andrew Chen hunched at desks looked up then. So Jasper has fixed it so Grace will stay on the one case, Winter's murder, only.

The article describes Irish mercenaries or collaborators teaching the Colombians urban guerrilla operations ("'It is worrisome because if there really is training in explosives, there is a concern that the conflict in the cities could spiral downward,' said Antonio Borrero, a security advisor and former rebel with the M-19 group... said he believed that the development was a sign that the rebels, a peasant-based organization that has mounted few military strikes in Colombia's cities, were trying to reach the cities in a well-planned strategy to continue debilitating the state.").

Below this article is another article, titled "I.R.A. Withdraws Its Disarmament Proposal" in talks with Britain. The top article links the arrest in Bogotá of the three I.R.A. bomb experts to cocaine trafficking ("Tests done on their clothing turned up traces of various kinds of explosives, officials said, as well as cocaine, which some government officials accuse the rebels of trafficking").

There's a brief history of the training of Colombian rebel or paramilitary groups by foreign terrorist organizations or mercenaries:

"In the 1980's Israeli mercenaries trained illegal antiguerrilla militias, right-wing groups that have accounted for the vast majority of massacres in Colombia.

"A now-defunct leftist rebel group, the M-19, had tight bonds with supporters outside Colombia and was believed to have contracted with Libyans to bring in arms shipments.

"Reports have also surfaced over the years that E.T.A., the Basque separatist group known for bombings in Spain, has worked with Colombian rebels.

"The Irish tie, if true, would signal the first time the Revolutionary Armed Forces of Colombia, or FARC, have established links with radical movements outside Latin America."

Grace had emerged from Captain Jasper Frank's office his dove-sagging lids still softly lowered as he murmurs Grace, you're doing a good job but this belongs to the Feds.

Seated beside her across from Captain Jasper Frank, the aging elephant wilting in the light who's standing pulling the blinds to half close them, shades Antonio Borrero who shakes Grace's hand. Borrero's eyes look in her eyes but she bends.

Grace small slender with long shining black hair hanging below her hip, eyes clear and dark asks Are the boys Colombian, who are they, are their deaths related to TOR dot.com?

Grace and Andrew had stooped over the corpses. Boys who fell or were pushed have jacks in them. They were being contacted and maybe directed. The jack had been inserted in the back of the necks.

Did you get the report back from forensics? Their mitochondrial and Y chromosome sequences fall outside contemporary lineages.

They *can't* be outside contemporary lineages, people. They *are*.

Strong, the horse in the rain when he's wounded, she's wounded—he steadies for her, holding his back which drifts in the rain in the field where they are. He's soaked, she's holding onto his soaked back steadied by it. Antonio's back drifts and then shifts to steady her. The high wind in the field, the horses' tails lash in it nearby them.

Borrero smiles his scent barely perceptible envelopes her, his trunk still as if his chest were shirtless—she hesitates—Detective Abe, you're very able. The connections, which I can't discuss are outside of San Francisco jurisdiction. When I've concluded my work here with your federal bureau, I'll give you as much information about it as possible, he nods politely.

Abe resumes the investigation of the death of Jonah Winter.

Sitting digging in her purse, Detective Abe says What do we have on Winter and Inventions dot.com? Well, Andrew begins, it's not pornography. Most of the dot.com companies that acquire information have gone under, but this one is making huge profits. They don't list all profits. He's excited. I hacked into their computer system last night. There are a string of links which lead to other dot.com companies or other kinds of businesses. Clothing, restaurants, but all listing huge profits. He's laying out pages for Grace and Cloe as he speaks. You think money laundering, Grace quiets. Some of these are big, legitimate corporations which here show huge profits received *from* Inventions dot.com. Some of the small businesses, they're carefully set up on paper, but this one, for example, storefront probably running at a loss if at all—if you look at its size, layout and location, I drove by there early this morning. But you see here, it lists a very high monthly income. They may all be hiding profits related to Inventions dot.com. Cloe and Grace stare at the pages of lists he's laid out for them. Why, this may be into billions, Cloe whispers.

But seated in the offices of Inventions dot.com again, waited on by the secretary Barbara Lord, there are no unusual amounts now in the accounts of any of the companies that are their contacts or operations. The money has passed through the screen swallowed leaving no record. Couldn't you retrieve it? to Andrew. Jockey, he's working on a ghost silent. Winter.

He died six days ago.

Whitened creased owl prim moves in and out. Phil, the third partner, drifts averted. But they're assisted by Barbara Lord, brisk crisply sweet. She's a dish-water blond hair and attire arranged efficiently. The office is silent with the prim owl gone then. Mr. Winter received a visitor several times who seemed strange, something odd, the last time was the day he died, the secretary offers. Grace and Andrew wait. He just dropped in, no appointments, I wasn't informed. But Mr. Winter seemed not to be expecting him and said before he closed his office door Why did you come *here?*—When? asks Grace—The day he died. The man had a full leathery hard face/mouth, a lot of red hair, no beard. He was wearing rough casual clothes. His manner hard and he didn't say anything. She pauses. I've worked for Mr. Winter for five years. He married Mrs. Winter four years ago and there's been a change. As if he's crushed, she's crushed him (she's says quietly)—so it would be hard to tell if his manner had changed from that or he was under tension from something else. But he was tense or short-tempered with the visitor, familiar with him. He snapped at him. Not a cringing manner. When were the other visits? Two different days last week, same thing he just came in.

Mrs. Winter, did your husband get along with his business partners? Yes, she says elegantly. She's composed now, slender in a black sweater and skirt here and there black-sequined. Wonder if nothing could move that expression, Grace muses. Her lips pressed elegantly, you wouldn't think her husband was a boiled pink shrimp? But Dahlia Winter views Grace Abe the inappropriate use of violence which has never occurred but as if it is unborn, an inappropriate person somewhere by one's nature a condensation like a pressed bead. Before it's occurred. Searching for it the pressed bead would materialize condensed between layers that are only Dahlia's haughty cold of wild ice.

Were you seeing someone else? I don't think that's any of your business. But no. Are you aware that your husband was involved in money laundering? In what? That's illegal, Grace quips. I don't know what you're talking about, I was not involved with my husband's work. But this doesn't concern you if he was doing so? Detective, I am suffering from grief, I'm very private. If you'll excuse me, I don't want to talk to you, she rises. I'm sorry, you *have* to talk to me. You won't leave? Dahlia's face is flexing a blue ice field with behind it more ice. Also fury, Grace talks to herself. A person *seeing* her angry has to be killed? wonders Grace. Uh, Officer Andrew Chen hesitates softly.

But obviously, Dahlia's lips tremble flexing moderated, accusing, I want to help. She smoothes her skirt, then sits. We will need to go through your financial accounts. Dahlia does not demur or change expression then, her face a mask without tension even. Except for that exchange with Grace, Grace's past. No further thought.

Andrew and Grace work on the Winter's bank statements silently taking notes. A worm hanging on a thread in the air comes between them. Featureless translucent pink, it floats near their bent heads. While the woman remains motionless on the sofa as if shocked about something. No one speaks.

She couldn't possibly regret because there's no relation between her and what happens. Not that regret would have anything to do with it?

Dahlia Winter had seethed, her face breaking up flexing, only past at present. Her face restrained by the thin lips, she hates, not realizing that is minor also. So it sweeps her as if carried in immense energy of wind outside—sunset, Grace imagines then, wanting to say to Dahlia Hating is repeated (except that would be misunderstood). She'd only conceive of Grace as hating. So that not perceiving hatred, or hers, she's carried, now a cocoon apart never meeting anyone. Can't meet Jonah Winter either before or now. At night taken within the fish by a wave. Though something is impinging. Who is thinking this? (Obviously, here. But that's not what I mean.) It's being thought somewhere in this—either ahead (before her) of her (by her?)—somewhere creating as a formed whole, that is visible at any time at once. That it might become, it's flat.

So their thought is is it connected to any action at all. Grace's thing is—she didn't know it would be repeated, until now. She was always innocent of occurrence, is now. Sees only occurrences.

Officer Cloe O'Brien has checked out a number of the locations listed by Andrew when she finally gets to Jackie's, a diner on Clement. Small, a few stools at the counter bar, a few tables. Brownies, some slices of pie. She orders a cappuccino, then sits in the police uniform while he's making it. Sighs.

A large, tall man shoulders in a worn leather jacket is at a counter stool, there isn't anyone else in the place. The first thing in her consciousness hearing the end of a sentence, he's Irish. From Dublin? she asks, her voice soft on the smile touching her face. Her small mother-of-pearl ears and spike-hair on head poised on a creamy neck float—even with where he turns on the stool the lip in a half smile at first. Then broader. Righto. You? Before I was born, she quips, tired. He's having a coffee, pays and rises, the heavy jaw moves on his blue eyes as he's still looking at her. You do a good business here, she means the guy making the cappuccino—who doesn't respond. For being here a short time, your books show you're making a killing. He looks uninterested if noticing—I wouldn't know. Cloe and the big man with the jaw nod, and at the side of her eyelids there's the impression of his large height leaving with his red hair seen outside the doorway then.

She walks down the street. Dumps the coffee in a Styrofoam cup taking it with her and follows him. I don't think so. He doesn't say anything but he doesn't think so, has put a rod into her back below the chest cavity where it meets the hip. You're going to shoot an officer? Stay turned. You're James Monaghan's brother, Timothy. I.R.A. Your brother was in the news. Stay turned. Then he was gone. Nowhere. She's looking running.

After a while, she's back at Jackie's but the guy serving insists The man comes in and waits around, the past few days. Just has coffee and waits around.

Cloe's going to Zuni's fast, the car in a sludge of traffic slow and cool grey fog, August evening. Parks to meet Grace and Andrew for dinner at 6:00. It's cold and she holds her jacket zipping it, feeling her breast plate beneath the soft erect bosom. Locking the car door street-side on Market in the wind a few homeless in doorways near her—there's a brown boy, about fourteen years old, by her—her bent side locking the car door before she sees him at her shoulder. The one who'd run from her when she showed him the photos.

My friends? he says as she turns gently to him. A thin beginning of a moustache above his upper lip. I want to talk to you but not here—can you come at Dolores Park tomorrow morning, 5:00? The officer answers, All right—there's a man who's handling this case. His name is Antonio Borrero. Is it all right if

I tell him and bring him to the park? I want to talk to *you*. *I'll* bring him.

Borrero? He's Colombian? He looks dubious. All right, the boy says and walks off in the grey, his collar pulled up.

It's 'like' sometimes you can grasp a nature, is it only hindsight? or the whole. Then. At once. Andrew is speaking leaning back in a fairly straight chair at Zuni's (waiting for a table), plays with his glass of scotch. *When?* Grace says laughing—*when* do you grasp the whole nature (of a person at once) in a present instant (by seeing) but is it hindsight even if you'd never met the person before and it's a very simple sight accurately? The whole, is only simple then. She's got a glass of Johnnie Walker also, she's just sipped, and Cloe O'Brien comes in.

Cloe's slow clear from the cool outside on Market Street (meeting the red beefy Timothy Monaghan, who is thinking A cop in San Francisco recognizes pictures from the terrorist list that's put out, that's how she knew—she's thinking One shot in the thorax or head, no one'd know he was here) comes into Zuni's, that's a wedge-shaped restaurant glass windows on the Market Street side where outside they keep the oysters on ice in buckets. Evening's coming down cool the homeless guys close on the rim of evening and cold Market yet Zuni's is at peace with that, accepting? or benign giving something to evening.

The computer has a function that normalizes language, all the sentence structure, Andrew is continuing. So? You turn it off, turn off that function, says Grace. Fundamentalists saying that nothing could occur by chance—everything is in the mind of God before—nothing could occur, Andrew exclaims.

Yes? Grace says taking a sip, on her throat then melodious, her long shining black hair loose draped on the chair.

In that there *is* occurrence. So the fundamentalists are trying to quash Science (they say Science) claiming it purports to have Truth, while it doesn't *purport* anything. Looks.

The length of the wall of windows riding beside Market Street, day and night are boats. The length of the wedge-shaped Zuni's, the tip is on a corner.

It is the boat of evening now.

Grace shifts her slender legs. Then sees Antonio Borrero leaning on the bar ordering.

She's beside him, walked to him from their bar table, where they're waiting to get a dinner table. Cloe's abstracted sitting in the background—a man steering her by holding her ears pulling gently the whole flesh frame as he's coming, between her legs on her and holding her cupping. As if the ears were flesh of one's and his, her having come after, when he is.

Cloe thinks. Interrupted. Detective Abe has brought back Antonio Borrero, who inclines his head politely, moving his drink in on the table as he sits down. Cloe says I met someone who can maybe help you with your case, and she tells him (the others looking interested. Also about Timothy Monaghan, then they all are blown). Borrero had been a member of the rebel group M-19 so Grace is curious, interested, not knowing anything about M-19 but light on him.

Or sweet on him, Cloe thinks and beams.

(Which is *not* what science does, investigating does *not* create a Truth. Andrew continues.)

While sleeping in black night folds is close to seeing the tiny children swim in day. The tiny mints (people-minnows?) swim with delicate curled backs. At night the guerrillas heard hunt for wild game with machine guns, the bursts floating in the air. Lost in the high black grass hearing them firing while they hunt. The boats coming up to the dock, tiny children swim in that no one travels at night. There is a river curfew. Outside, except for a tin roof under which the cocoons are strung floated lines in the vast slabs of black rain in night falling in which there's a moon. Seated at the table here and lying in the hot night hangs as a cocoon with lines of cocoons. Being that's in public, he has a reverie that's 'at the same time.' So that, stilled by being with others, he can reflect.

Would you like to try this? Grace offers him a taste of her Ahi tuna. But behind this is a coil at the back of which she changed. Instead of floating with her and someone else *as* her, the two caused to materialize by a moment, a pause out of which she and someone else in her, a marine/a particular person who had lived outside her (ghosting) would (sequentially, again and again) float out—she sees him outside her. He doesn't have someone floating in him, only him at the same time in him. They are clear and rest.

Realism is seen to be the minute one only in movement, as of one's lovers and friends. Or movement. He's between only being in himself, without some particular other person being him at the same time in him, and 'to be events in the huge outside.'

A bicycle is in the blur of darkness outside Zuni's windows. That border Market Street.

The Indians are really slaves, now. They work for the drug growers—his face is becoming tight, his voice quieter but tense, either to weep or be in rage as they are similar. Their not being far apart is appearance. Or determination. Determination could be related to tears or rage, or alongside.

Do you think, Cloe asks, that the journalist was paid to create the story—by drug growers or government? Antonio Borrero collects himself and then shrugs. Softly, I don't know. It's possible (not specifying which).

And, out of disappointment, gumming him (Jonah Winter), held in her mouth, where eating him alive—gumming him as if she's aged—she feels bitter tears spurt and feels the tears mix with the ball she's gumming.

They're outside of Zuni's leaving on the sidewalk of cool night. Storefronts of Market behind trolley tracks on the street below moon, cars pass. A car, a blur passes a drive-by shooting. From the point of view of the passerby, a car beside theirs (some other car from which this is seen) drives by Zuni's. At the corner shots come from the blurred car and a man standing at the corner staggers. He falls when the blur is gone (when the car is not visible). The driver in whose iris the scene occurs cries out in his (a passerby's) car.

The blur car from which the shots rained, pumping five shots at the pavement and the people passes and glides down Market. Fires from a darkening blur.

It was Antonio Borrero who fell. He dived hit, the others beside him standing drawing guns.

Because the flesh is only present-time—occurs only there—and is romanticism, being simply different—the flesh is left out in actions. Yet Grace remembers making love with Antonio Borrero.

The relation of character to action.

Nothing occurs in speaking or in its communing then. It is separate. Pete Debree who has a lazy soul has no action either. That is the same, sloth. Though he plays (tennis) but he is otherwise separate from motion, and friendly alert still there isn't extension, not communing with anyone though there with them. The moment in which he might commune with Grace Abe is there, but facetious charm really stinging sees her be nothing, rather than that one devoted be brought to that or seen in that. He doesn't think there's that to which one is devoted. Action is communing only—so this would be where movement is not speaking or inside, or outside only. But he won't come to that ever. She misses that with him even, but he does not miss it? Ever? So that's also not communing?

And he can't see that his partner has died because something can't occur (in his way of seeing)—yet something *has* occurred, so that action isn't communing either.

Can't? Can't be closed. Mabel Jet is speaking, that's not what she says (about Dahlia) or in her speech, it's a rush there. Mabel Jet calls.

She calls worried, urgent. Rushes talk, critical. Grace in early morning goes to Dahlia Winter's apartment where the door is opened by Mabel Jet who says to her She Dahlia wouldn't ever hurt anyone. But Grace thinks then Mabel Jet may be warm, vivid, sensual without observing anyone ever—that one would be Dahlia Winter's friend is dependent on not observing? But no observation isn't the friend. Both dependent on that. Mabel Jet talking a rush of warmth without sight. Dahlia has disappeared since last night, says Mabel Jet, fearing something may have happened to her when she met someone. Who did she meet? I don't know, he is someone Jonah had business with, and Dahlia wanted to finish it so she could be paid. Now I'm afraid because she didn't come home. She doesn't usually know anything about his work. Grace goes right to Pete Debree.

Officer Cloe O'Brien walks into the park at Dolores Street at ten to 5:00 AM to meet the boy. She enters alone but Andrew is nearby crouched with the border of parked cars concealing him from inside the park. But outside he is visible. The park bordered by apartment houses quiet and quiet trolley tracks above the grassy knoll which is open and grey, the boy is standing in the grass. Cloe walks to him.

The relation of character to action is horizontal. Pete Debree comes in to meet Grace Abe at his office early. Debree's unlocking the outside door—they're in the hall, the charming, distanced alert hawk already with her, states he hasn't seen Dahlia—and the reception room is a mess. Silently, they go through into his office, in which files and papers are open and strewn on the floor and sofa. Amidst these on the floor the whitened creased mussed fluffed dried stiffened owl of Melinka lies with a bullet hole in his chest visible in a pool of blood, Melinka his wife. And Pete Debree looks at a loss for a while, puzzled but without a strong reaction, relinquishing it to her.

18. THE WEDGE

It can't be 'our' 'happiness.' One's own appearance is *as* outside only, inside having been consumed by the worm-pod-flower.

Destroys the inside of others—by displacing 'one's' experiencing and 'one's' theorizing that both.

"I *am* the business" is said by the Replicant who learns her identity having thought she was human (in *Blade Runner*). 'Not recognizing that one is constructed' is the capitalist-business. It displaces actual outside event, redefining history, obliterating those past and current events.

In waking at night ('state' in) terror that one (young adult) 'hadn't lived' 'was not living' *then* at that instant at night (it is impossible to do so ever)

before terror is subject to the experience *there*—the experience is something else.

Exterior/interiorized event (both) 'is' unformed only (by one?)—nor is terror a cause of it (is before it, after it).

That 'it's not causal' is characteristic of terror—it's by itself and may not have an effect on 'crowds that are in violence (so it's outside one while one's there).'

Is there any place 'where' (when) there could be motion?

If one's liked that's a 'thing' itself. Others are re-formed to like one, if one's doing that.

"That's what it is to be a slave." 'But the only way of being outside.' In total change, the butterfly has no memory as it's structurally totally different.

The boys, slaves from an off-world colony, thrown (or who'd thrown themselves) ruffled float air currents falling amid the skyscrapers. Their being derived from imported children, they don't resemble adults (as if not derived from them). Only that child-strain prevails, as them. To transform across both sides of the barrier. That is interior also.

These children's nature (their physical being when alive) *is* the reflection the outside here transformed. Their being reflection only is here quickly and in the dull beads in the children after death.

'Written' is secret. Vision occurs by it being written.

While the butterfly and its worm are at once, superimposed as each other, only? throughout one entirely, *then?* relation of 'the inside of the inside' to dying—or 'the outside to one' to dying.

It's qualified everywhere. Eating the mango. Seeing T singing.

"Dependent origination" itself (that occurrences are interactive, have no independent being, as described by Nāgārjuna) is itself also illusion. (Nāgārjuna's logic would concur with this.)

*Example, interpretation of Nāgārjuna's logic: roses only qualify the rose horizon. As such they are two separate things: in that anything seen 'from' oneself is only in that one moment (which isn't existing either, that moment or oneself then), is 'only' 'composed.' The roses are not related to a rose horizon inherently, in that they are dependent on one seeing them in that way at an instant. One also doesn't exist 'as that,' not inherent as that one seeing (who is not separate in memory, but is dependent on that instant existence of the roses). An occurrence is not separate in existence, is *then* inherently empty in not having any instant.

Related to everything else, things are falling apart.

one fairly young man says Even—young people don't see they have any part of this—are letting it go. they don't make anything either. or see any reason to—such as: *the breath on the cycle downtown and the clear spring entire day, that boy riding—making that.*

Like folded on a wave inside of which Esau de Light flies dropping onto the street the cycle cresting the steep hill landing touching after taking off from it, he races on.

Some girls who are forced prostituted are walking on the street getting some light, out in it.

Cloe passing, Esau de Light speeds to her, retching to a stop the cycle beating so Cloe looking up thinks of a panther as the eyes break into a smile which the patches of blonde hair stick tufts into the light around the jack in the back of his head.

Made it, he says, apparently referring to her, she infers, meaning the other day, when they'd parted abruptly flying off the cycle and running instead from the pimp.

Cloe still rubs her bruises. She's still for an instant and returns his slow smile.

A sound apparently enters his head from the jack because the expression in his eyes changes, registered by the jaw saying to Cloe, Got to go.

She doesn't know whether he means her or him.

Something's coming over the hill (it's San Francisco) Esau de Light's just crested. Esau de Light says nothing but his eyes look frantic in his jaw.

What are you afraid of? she implores knowing it's a stupid question.

But he's gone on the cycle.

19. TIME FLATTENED

The creases in many layers, the little pert mouth in creases, a pool of blood on his shirt—she thinks of him as a Peruvian feather dress. Especially when he's powdered, for prints. Thoughts are just on the surface.

The whitened pert Phil Wilson, many creases everywhere, was buried that day. His wife Melinka in hat and gloves that held a purse and kept opening it digging through it, wept on a slightly leathery face, the eyes puffed. The eyes holding back tears, then they pour down her face before she's had time to dig the purse for the Kleenex.

A homeless person is found dead, strangled left on the grounds outside a church.

Writing, which *is* time (being in it), to terminate time is to expand it, conceptual-physiological time, though 'physiological' as being is different from 'writing' as being—*so that these are the same*. (Such an episode—recently a homeless person was killed— is in the newspaper.)

> In the high-altitude passes. Traveling higher and higher, unable to breathe finally. At night held a huge bag of oxygen, clutching with body that is curled on the bag. Attached by a tube into the nose, rib cage expanding from it all night, even the rib cage slept.

Windsurfing looks like butterflies with one wing. Expanding on the wing. Or termites flying cling to their one wing. Clinging to the oxygen in passes is Para surfing: a shell (like a quarter) of a parachute lifts the figure who's skipping and he sleds racing the water, the ocean hanging beneath the shell of parachute so that the person is hurled on the whole ocean and wafted by wind. A confabulation of Para surfers dash the vast blue water—

on mid-sea the waves are not breaking—so that the people are careening on the heavy blue sheet pulled by the shells of parachutes, the ocean hanging on (or moved by) the sky.

When these are the same (being)—is a state of bliss, everyday. One *does* it, in physiological time. They exist at once and don't interfere with each other. There time is thin, wide, the present, past, future—existing at once, and don't interfere with each other.

Grace and Andrew go after Pete Debree, interrogating him, and opening for review all of his files. Debree tires sometimes but usually is puzzled, deftly caustic, yet patient also as if he has nothing to hide.

Antonio wounded (a bullet in the left leg) which later aches, disappears. Is staying at Grace's apartment, without telling his whereabouts to the Feds or police (except Frank's officers). Recovering, he's also going over the boxes of Debree's files. But no trace has been left of the passage of funds between Inventions dot.com and the other businesses. They have to be silent. (He'd made love to her with the bit, the stick, between his teeth, in order not to make a sound there.) I think, Borrero writes on a notepad to Grace in the second evening, Inventions may be using all of the companies on Andrew's list—or all of the companies using *them*, he's wearily thinking—which gives these 'legitimate' corporations huge profits from what source? A separate army or empire, separate from and the same as your legal force. Grace says, Which is an investigation that's outside our level.

Having joined the itinerant crowd, of homeless, living amongst them, they are unprotected. Five more boys are killed. Some shot when they are running, found in separate locations, their limbs flung in a posture of flight. All have the jack inserted in the back of their necks. They are identified by homeless people on the street, who'd assumed they were abandoned or runaways as anonymous others. So only the faces are remembered as if glimpses.

Blasting led by the nose. Mabel Jet keeps calling Grace. Mabel Jet is stressed, rushed in speech, always seeing as how the other people around her see because the local is all that exists. Not even to wonder what someone is like? A full-bodied woman beautiful in large hats and sashes, child-and-husband-absorbed, loyal, warm without attention, except Dahlia's missing. It's not that she doesn't act but within that pool her tyranny omitting attention blithely assuming another is worthless without looking hurting them ramming along for someone else carried by the blithe warmth caustic (so it's *not* warmth? when did that take place?) even were Dahlia not missing, or were Dahlia not there, the difference in one's nature would start her *not to* (listen) even?…conveying the hearer either nonexistent or 'only their ego' *whereas* Dahlia… Anyway she's not seeing Dahlia. The police are looking for the missing Dahlia, Grace explains. Which they are, stretched thin. That's on the surface wild ice—wild ice isn't buried. And here time is thin, wide.

The Inventions dot.com secretary, Barbara Lord, has been replaced. Probably because she offered information to the police. The replacement is Emilia Hart who's in her late twenties/early thirties married frozen in an adolescent attachment to her parents (and thus her new employer somehow) with the sense that the interviewers should praise her in speaking and be in reference to her own parents who are implicitly praised also when Emilia is receiving a coded description of herself as if the interviewers speaking are authorities/that is *mothers but who therefore are also nothing.*

The young Emilia rebukes with the increasingly middle-aged skin right then (in that instant as she rebukes)—for Grace asking a point of information about the files had not led with praise from a reference first obliquely to Emilia's parents—the young woman retorting You're hostile, I don't want to speak to you. You *have* to speak to me, Grace steels replying.

Antonio Borrero, dark hair, fine hair of moustache. In M-19, as a boy. From fairly wealthy family not corrupt. They had died (circumstances not given). He left their life then. Is also a man in M-19. The rebel group is now defunct. That's all there is on him, Captain Jasper Frank says and leans back dove-lids sagging on the stubbled jowls as he crouches backward in the tilted chair in his office remarking It's coming from the Feds anyway. Trust no one, he remarks dryly stuffing an unlighted cigarette in the side of his mouth, then yanking it out where it's seen on the desk.

He's been there all night working. Damn it, dove-lids says, getting up and moving from his office chair in the slanted light of the slatted blinds. He catches a butterfly, gently cups it in his huge paws and releases it through the window that's open behind the blinds. He returns to his chair, the unlit cigarette now perched in his jowls. Trying to quit, he says sheepishly, finding Grace's gently smiling at him.

Three more boys are shot down, a wandering drive-by on Van Ness. But the killer, after shooting got out of the car. The jacks were extracted from the boys' necks. The killer pulled the jacks, leaving empty holes.

The others pause in a combination of horror which is even puzzlement, Cloe saying softly *Like mutilation?*

The janitress at TORRID dot.com, who'd vouched to seeing one of the boys jump from the window, calls Grace at her office. Says she didn't see the boy.

She had to say she saw him jump.

Who made you say this, who spoke to you? Grace asks. There's silence. Grace sees on her retina the flustered woman. Where are you? I will come to you.

By the time Grace gets there, the woman found in an alley is dead, a jack in the back of her head pulled.

Captain Jasper Frank's fist hammers down on his desk, he's shouting. Or raising his voice. In his closed office. Sequestered with the chief, Chief Demurgent who is emphasizing that emigrants don't have the rights of citizens, he harangues, they can be arrested and detained indefinitely, their rights have been taken away from them. But we don't *have* one of them, alive! Jasper Frank rejoins exasperated, yet evasively. The fist hammers only one time but a murmur of the two voices floats into the hall. After a while, Chief Demurgent moves up the hall puckering his face a little.

In that evening Grace has a reverie—she's walking, Antonio Borrero is dressing his wound, as he does; leg extended, seated on the edge of the bed. He reminds her of her, though he's serene. She races out of her skin. Young she'd trembling tensed geared, running had applied the drug to the burn marks. She had velvet firm flesh in steely knots. His hand massaging the wing bones of her back holds her rib cage as if it'd been released in the previous night.

Lying on his chest, they're on the edge, a rounded side of the cliff of white shining bright grass at night facing that night everywhere where they are staying the same (utterly not insensate) compared to that huge 'night not insensate.'

But when Grace is speaking to the Captain she'd already e-mailed Colombian officials and the American Embassy in Bogotá for information about and description of members of FARC. She does not mention this to Captain Jasper Frank. Inadvertently, she's learned that Antonio Borrero is still in Bogotá. The man passing for Borrero in San Francisco is someone else unknown.

The dead boys have no lineage. Or are outside of contemporary lineage. Having the same physical appearance, of boys, while interiorly not related to any existing adults, are no one's children, the jacks implanted in the back of their necks by drivers plugging them into functions they're compelled to do or information they transport?

....

Sometime there has got to have been the instance when Cloe released the turtle, smashed the glass tank in the market.

Cloe puts the turtle in the bath. The turtle Hazel moves out of her hands into the light water that's become the tub from the light coming into the bath water in her apartment.

Cloe worries about how she's going to care for it in the future—then laughs, thinking of the amber-hump on the tiny aged lady walking. The body in solitude bathes. Except it's night.

The amber-hump out gets clouded by some passing robes blowing harnessed so the amber-hump is inside one of the robes now, for a moment. It's filled with excruciating pain dying but that's nothing *then* even. While it's going on, it's not so bad.

A jackhammer begins in the street. Water she'd drunk feels her throat still as much as she does as she has no reason to feel everything or to worry about filling it either, she sleeps, the dark lights panting in the day ahead still.

20. AS JOY SPATIAL-CROWD-ONLY AND THAT EXISTS 'AS' ONE'S INNER LIFE ALSO

A conclusion first: It is a military present. Oneself (as being 'theorizing,' and 'experience' as that) can only 'be' by escaping off-world colonies and world; that is, by actual action. Now. Inside the relation, or being the relation only, that is between conceptual and world.

Cloe steps from the shower, bends and with the towel dries a soft cream-colored long muscular leg. She stands from bending, the flesh of the breasts upright then, and from nowhere a small flesh-colored translucent lizard leaps and lands on her belly. This happened to me. It's random memory. It doesn't use its delicate flesh-legs, wingless; yet flies up again, holds to her breast. She doesn't cry out but brushes it with the towel into a part of the towel, places it in a paper bag in which she punches tiny holes. To release this flesh-colored thing outside.

Cloe's man hands her a cup of coffee through the bathroom door. The steam passes through the crack of the open door, his hand there holds the cup.

Remembers while walking on the street where an elephant's trunk between her legs (his trunk removed outside her—is— then he puts it in again) out in day so that it's dragged through her legs, which closed on a hose—an elephant's trunk that dragged she's standing through her legs, she walks some, helping.

The ocean is the same as the night and the day. Rolls of the black clouds racing a hanging wedge is black in rain, the ocean. And the wedge falling not shifting the day, the night not moving though racing falls as ocean then. Only then coinciding, yet the wedge doesn't exist ever separately. One is moving awake small under huge hanging wedge in black of black racing white not moving much which is huge at night.

Captain Jasper Frank has bought flowers and groceries. Fumbles in the hall for his apartment door key, while he's holding the brown bags, the wedge falling black outside slabs bouncing off the sidewalks audibly. Damn it, he thinks the bulb has burned out, just thinking, when there's a blast that flashes inside his chest trunk flattening him against the wall, smashes him back first hitting a can amid the brown bag held to his chest while the groceries are spraying the wall. Where he's fumbling in the dark entirely exposed and illumined by the night lamp outside, he finds his holster and is sent blasting back with another wallop. A pump bursting in him, he shoots and shoots.

Cloe O'Brien's flesh-colored nude form emerged from the shower, the black slabs racing and falling filling the streets outside bounce. She gently removes a small colored translucent lizard clinging to her similarly soft, clean flesh before dressing. Emerging into the black sidewalk which while illumined is submerged in the slabs that, covering a car parked across from her form, squeeze a flash in their black folds bouncing the side of the building. She darts crouching soaked firing in black. Then clings to the corner of the building firing, the car like a settled module bouncing minutely in the falling black clouds of rain.

Barely wheezing breathing in the hallway of Grace Abe's apartment building, where, her door open, a thin tall figure is visible which crouches then dangling in the open window leaves through it to the fire escape scaffolding, behind the figure Jasper Frank breathing heavily fires breaking the windows chipping the walls in that he's first seen a figure on the floor of the dark room. When it's turned, the figure is Antonio Borrero holding his gun. His belly is bleeding. He dies later at the hospital during an operation, transported to the hospital in a taxi by Jasper Frank who's bleeding heavily, but who lives.

Cloe O'Brien is crawling nimbly on the scaffolding that clings to the shell of Andrew's building in the bouncing black folds. The black falling slabs submerge and pass her in the air as she crawls on the skeleton scaffolding clinging to his window. Andrew meets her and opens the window. He's shot something that's on the sofa. She left one which fell in the falling racing slabs of rain that are bouncing off the scaffolding. But when Andrew and Cloe descend to the street by the stairs within the building, the body which had fallen past her from the scaffolding isn't on the ground. They're running checking the lines of empty cars in the rain. Nothing moves.

21. MELINKA'S OWL

Take Mabel Jet. Animal warmth is there but not contemplation—not capacity for contemplation in the cells? so that a political movement might coerce her to have seemed to change but only 'to talk the talk,' that that would then *be* change, outside. It is. Change not occurring inside her... *Others see that simply.* The conceptual structure is entirely separate from the physical structure. It's all right to say anything because no one cares.

Grace's careening in the car. Her heart has flown into her throat. She's been ignorant. But it's so serious it's not even self-castigation—she simply sees (feeling this as an aftermath) The subjective interior *is* alleviated—of one—in life by change inside. His dying is in this time, but not in the future. Yet she has missed him. The blind one gets angry (sees it as true), she thinks—doesn't even think that's anger—Someone spat, many people spitting, so the mole holds to 'changing their character.' Then, they don't change. Ever. Before, either. It's only one regarding 'seeing the relation of character to action' all as 'trying to see character (theirs) at all.' Weighing motions coming at its blind side. But the outside huge. As if character and my seeing caused something, neither do—or, known, *these* are simple anyway. Just there. There's a connection which I don't see, not seeing is repeated continually. Character is always invisible to me. Since character won't change anyway, the days are in themselves, dropped. Always. The moon drops below every day now. They're at once moons and days crossing a line. My attending to the character of others as if anyone's capable of not being itself (or that it isn't that at first even) is omitting attention, yet how *not* try to figure them out? But I'm in front of someone and don't see anything, that is my nature. Driving in between big rigs that are hauling ass so fast and not even able to see Borrero has been swept away, passed when seeing him being swept *(My illusion that I can change character/it can change completely—is not shared by the community, it's illusion,* really. *I just keep doing that/not seeing people or myself, without knowing it, and I won't necessarily change now either whatever I do. To see this trait as oneself even only lasts for an instant. I'll forget. can't live ever)* Grace weeps (is *'seeing'* 'oneself'? It's intention in the white grass). She's crouched in the rain on a fire escape scaffolding of Melinka's apartment, peering in the window at Melinka on the sofa in conversation with two thin men with rope-muscles, holding a pistol on Melinka who's seated knees together crying under her little dry mat of dyed chestnut-colored hair digging her purse for Kleenex, so one man tears her arm. Grace's earlier entered the hospital where Jasper Frank is being treated and Antonio last lost his life fleeing in the rain—Grace squints in it. The short Melinka bends to pick up the purse which knocked from her lap almost falls by a coffee-table leg. Then after she bends the man boxes Melinka, a hit to the side of her small face and she pitches. He cuffs her again. So Grace unleashes a stream of fire chipping the lights and walls, pinning the people a halo around the short weeping Melinka sometimes illumined unmoving in it. When Grace enters the room, jumping in from the window, the men have retreated and Melinka still sits on the sofa. Though now she's not crying, converses briefly, rises and from her deep purse relinquishes Phil Wilson's small laptop to Grace. They'll return, Grace insists, touching her. But Melinka shrugs and remains behind. There's a photo in the room of her prim owl, her husband.

The M-19 had taken over the government building in the 1970's. The structure is pocked with shells. All the M-19 members who were in the siege were killed. However, they were bold. The group was successful in many raids. The group agreed later to lay down their arms and work with the government for a political solution. The FARC remains outside, drug dealing and kidnapping for funds. Yet the mass of the people are poor, killed, enslaved, still.

Not Melinka's owl. Who was a chief in FARC.

Antonio had grown up in a wild sleeping in a tree at night—
as a moon in the tree, the limbs of which plunged draped silent
in dark around illumined stars. Not knowing how to speak to
others, but which he does—without being taught, and as if being turned reverse first, backwards in that 'social' is not the objective (in the sense of, for anyone)—by not having this objective (of 'social' or speaking even) he is guided by birds in trees
and by trees to see people's kindness. And by stars to see one.

But this is cut off now, instantly in death. It seems impossible that there could be death if there's life, the infant instantly
in life.

So it's just no memory. Grace speaks to herself. She had
studied for/sought the fact of this kindness. But she herself will
soon be dead.

She is barred? Dahlia: Feeling doesn't open an iris which is
deep green but having changed is not questions, wasn't. Or study-
ing the iris carefully, one is unseen. That the person is custom-
driven isn't a description of them or that 'they are cold,' though
it may be true. There is no character (in any one) but it's also
visible in them. But it's a stream.

Kneeling drinking at the small stream.

22. NO LOST ACTIONS

In the dream, neither experiencing the pain nor 'seeing' the spine surgery of three weeks ago (lower back fused, a fist-sized plate of bone formed from a fracture is removed, spine bolted with titanium rods, Terminator), neither reliving nor description, my mind accessed 'being operated upon' fully awake, 'itself' is the entire being. A 'shallow' physiological frame, as that which is 'interior-subjective'—implies memory of everything at once is fiction.

I left this in there at the time I had the dream.

Dream had to have 'another operation,' actually the same one of three weeks ago—and I was going to it, in some kind of urban Mars, through clusters of figures embroiling one (in flight *towards* the spine surgery, with an old friend who is a doctor in real-time and asked innocent questions which is like her real nature). The dream was 'physiological remembrance' of the real spine surgery *as it occurring* by spatial sense, traveling. Though unconscious in the real-time event, under general anesthetic, I was aware in it. That is related to butterflies' complete metamorphosis. I was afraid in the dream because in it undergoing the operation-as-actual-memory or actual-event?

No Lost Actions, Pal Mal

Comics *won't be* interior. That's their characteristic. That they do not have that faculty or form. Theory of Pal Mal. Pal Mal comic is a space. Similar to circadian rhythm, the flesh's clock in which the sun shining on any cell in a person's body resets the person's waking rhythm to day.

It's the same as the spine's dream. It dreams/*is* the operation on itself, as traveling. A Mars but going toward it.

It was awake. Outside is the same as the Tibetans uncovering their mind formations, and being free in them—having to use even their own being tortured imprisoned denigrated transformed (by their torturers) to uncover their own minds *anyway*, their phenomena becoming the *means* of doing it.

On the small level, Grace says about friends M and P: I could perceive that they attack others and even then could penetrate that in its relation to their occurrence, be moved by them and as their configurations, loved them; but when they attacked me I could only see 'all of it later': *their action in all and one being in all* (one's actions in all) suddenly really. I'm disturbed that I have to be in it, as recipient only, in order to know it. It's not graspable by the mind only. Further, while perceiving this I don't hate them; but when there is a flicker of not perceiving this, I do hate them. So one's mind *is* acting (on it, and performing, is flesh) always.

Out of the top of a little red convertible headed by two blondes, tangles blowing on the red blur, which stops, emerges from the driver's side a burnt blonde buffalo-cake, flaps of cake hanging on him blotched a hue of red on the sides which are also tattooed. Tattooed with lightening stripes circling both hued arms, like bear limbs hanging under or from the tangled blonde tendrils that touch red-cake bulbous (shoulder-muscles). The buffalo-cake tattooed slabs. The blonde lady, on the passenger side of the little red convertible which blurring zipping, stopped there, stays in while he gets out and flexes the slabs. And the chunks hang on him, tattooed and red from the sun which is glinting off the flame trees too or flowering trees, jutting around them.

Grace laughs, a flash of teeth visible though she's feeling glum, the blonde advancing cake mirrors in her sunglasses. He's pulled over, now is coming back, and leans quizzically in the window of her rental, indicating there. Park there.

It's a laid-out Japanese villa perched on the black lava fields that are running into the Pacific, lime-green ice plants sprouting on the black fields, which it holds like a fortress. Behind them and encroaching on the red road on which they've entered is the high wild cane grass birds shooting over it fly straight toward them.

Racing the black rolls of clouds that move on the bright green cane grass, anyway shooting on the top of it. Some birds shoot off the backs of standing horses then, whose tails are swishing, lashing in the wind then.

Grace stands. Blonde-cake sways the tattoos ahead of her walking so they go in. Mr. Monty is not Japanese. The villa is formal, old—so she doesn't know whether he belongs here but that's irrelevant and she asks what she came to ask.

There've been some murders in San Francisco. One of our men killed also. Borrero? he's not one of yours. He's mine, she says simply. He nods, and looks at her politely. He's bought the place, the old upper-class Japanese family returned to Japan, she thinks.

Mr. Monty welcomes Detective Grace Abe's visit because he wants to be clear. He speaks carefully, coded but outlining. They're not his, he'll negotiate and contain them. It would be too wild otherwise, Grace trusts.

Earlier: Officer Cloe O'Brien entered the grass of the park on Dolores Street, Officer Andrew Chen on the other side of the parked cars surrounding the grass where she meets the boy who ran from the photographs of corpses of boys flown from buildings. The boy looks older than she thought. He says they work for some men, she nods, Colombian? He nods, But they're having trouble. What kind? They're getting killed (he gives the boys' names—One boy jumped. He didn't *jump*), we revolted, so we're being killed. They also wanted the men who are our boss we staged a rebellion from, but our bosses, our drivers, they got away. Who is they? He ignores that, is silent. Well, who are the killers? He enters conversation again, They're yours, army. Army, can't be, she doesn't believe him. Army, he says firmly, they're in Colombia working for both governments, they deal. What? Weapons and drugs, he says scorning her. She tries again, One of the men, is he big, tall, a lot of red hair. No, there's one with buzz cut, marine cut that's light brown hair, thin, strong man.[1]

They're couriers, of information and drugs. Slaves of or slaves used by the army here.

Seize one's own mind, one sees one's own mind (in the dream one's spine/mind being operated on—as if that's occurring 'from above'—is undergone only via or 'as' *other* events spatially. The 'operation' itself is without language or representation there).

Complete metamorphosis is total change, no relation between the physiological being of one in the larvae stage, and 'the same one' in the butterfly stage. 'No memory can cross' 'no allusion' *is* the 'conception' (birth) of it.

The 'exterior-only' is solely imagination (that isn't possible). 'Exterior-only' would not have memory then (that is allusion).

The pictures seen by the eye are always 'remembered' and are physiological sites (first, before apprehension); *are* allusions.

To write as 'only seeing on the retina'—where what one sees is not determined before, ever.

Complete metamorphosis is different from exterior. Have complete metamorphosis. Have come from that, impermanence. It is akin to 'memory of everything'—then being something that is entirely separate 'remembering'? As separation *itself*.[2]

But transformation on the physiological level (to machines) in *Terminator* has created a condition of only action, no inner life. There is only power (there is *their* exterior, destroying the interior of anything. And there is: they're not seeing that as they do it). Then this *leads* to 'one seeing outside.'

---

1. A time change. The I.R.A. teaching urban terrorist techniques in Colombia occurred in 2001, and was reported in the *New York Times* in that year. The action takes place at a later time, the times occurring here at the same time.

2. One is 'serial compartments,' like Treasure Discovery, each of the compartments is simultaneously or later accessed.

Faith is 'outside,' of either occurrence itself or oneself physiologically.

'Struggle' theorized in one as in the chrysalis is physiological-conceptual—(rather than psychological, which is composed/socially interpreted?).

Someone challenges the above argument, saying "Doubt is a co-participatory state of mind, whereas when one struggles,

---

A component of U.S. body snatchers, however, is the conception that physiological has no being. That which is the body and that which is the mind are separate and are blank. (See Kathy Acker.) And are the crowd. Unlike Walter Benjamin's view of the crowd as the subject being contemplated. Nothing is accessed in *Invasion of the Body Snatchers*, but is transformed.

Nāgārjuna's logic is structural, everything being impinged on in every moment of time. 'Dependent origination,' meaning that nothing has inherent being—memory occurs, events occur, but these are not the same thing ever. Nothing is even the same as itself *then* in any instant.

In *Terminator 2* the woman's continual rebellion against the reforming that's occurring of the subjective—once they change the exterior structure of future society—is no longer necessitated. The subjective interior *is* alleviated—of one—in life by change outside.

Therefore we are not bound to continual rebellion, except that in *Terminator 2* they find a moment and a place (the computer company at their present) in the frame of time which when changed changes everything that is later. It *can be* structural-logistic there.

Is (every) one's 'continual conceptual rebellion' here as the basis at any moment and place—changing the outside future structural? Only in 'one's' present? O, not at all in one's present?

'Interior' and 'structural' are false ordering. The machine, who loves the boy, kills itself so that the future already experienced will not occur. There will be no vestige, father, that originates that future—whereas *Invasion of the Body Snatchers* is only destruction of the present, at that present.

The boy in *The Sixth Sense* is "only a conduit" in that seeing and speaking to the dead who don't know they're not living he (loses his life) won't be living (as we perceive it)? People realizing they're 'only' conduits (that they don't have lives) are awake in having no illusory connections? Everything then is seen to be neither living nor dead, in fact. That is, everyone is *not* living in the conventional framework *in fact*.

Survival in *Terminator* depends on changed-actions (ones in the past, present, and future) restructuring the course of events. At first I thought this was superficial change. But it is 'akin' to fundamental restructuring, in that it touches on *physiological*.

one struggles against the flow; struggle is divisive—one struggles in separation from something (as a butterfly from the chrysalis?)."

This rational perception of struggle caused struggle in the one listening.

Doubt implies a rational 'ordering' since 'to doubt' is to be formed (aware of perceiving) and outside the subject? The task is to undo one's *seeing* at all.

If reason is the view of phenomena transpiring in an order that is socially conceived, reason is itself cause and effect, *is* that order? It obscures phenomena's relativity ('emptiness of occurrence'—of occurrence *being* 'our' ordering).

Complete metamorphosis '*isn't*' the relation between things.

"—one struggles in separation from something (as a butterfly from the chrysalis?)" The conflict 'doesn't make sense,' *and* is exactly what is expressed:

Seeking this separation, as the *means* of not being translated 'back.'

In one it is not even 'oppositional.' It is oppositional politically/socially. One thing is *not* transformed into another, ever. One is *already* outside.

Artaud explained some of his texts as manifestations of physiological aberration whereby what the mind is (at all) might be investigated. Said he was insane. He was proposing what his mind is outside of itself. In *The Theatre and Its Double*, the notion of gesture outside of language, implying 'pre' and 'post' language 'at once,' is thorough separation, the chrysalis not being the butterfly. One who is healthy also sees outside either (butterfly or chrysalis) by not being the separation even.

The barrier between the chrysalis and the butterfly (neither are independent)—is 'being dependent' *as* 'there being no entity' (either).

There isn't "flow" between chrysalis and butterfly either, if it's complete metamorphosis. There can't be continuum even.

The chrysalis struggles as a separate being with its later completely different 'self'—can't because that other 'self' isn't existing yet; this can occur only as 'contemplation'?—'contemplation' meaningless in that it is: not itself later because it bears no resemblance, no memory therefore.

The chrysalis is not allusion (even to struggle, or to *its* struggle, or to the butterfly)—except its written instructions?

This seems to account for one's experience. Especially intensity almost not remembering any physical actions, so words there are sensory I doubt (*now*) I can walk up the stairs is sensory.

Complete metamorphosis can't occur except the change being in the outside.

The notion of 'rigor' is merely a doctrine which changes what's seen. One can't approach the terrain (of any 'experience') with gentleness and inclusiveness (without frames) *until* having been drastic (a drastic change of oneself, hard on oneself and completely different from inclusiveness). Writing is: fictional itself producing/necessity of realistic change.

Doubt, faith, and rationality are not the vehicles or process of Tibetan *Secret Autobiography*. Only literal 'seeing' (sight) is.

23. THE FOOTNOTES

Dahlia isn't found. Dahlia's iris having motions.

After Grace's release from prison, Dahlia's fate obsesses Grace. Memories of the details of each time she'd seen Dahlia recur, only the order of these details varying. She starts looking for Dahlia on the basis of these memories. Grace even takes the drug Ibogaine again, depending on it for clarity (not of memory, but of the future). There, Grace can't even weep.

While going through the motions. So that (action) isn't communing either. No, it is. Kathy Acker proposes that her text *is* the other text.

One can get to Grace's character from Pete Debree. See the dainty hawk. Because she responds. One, from sloth, can't think to commune, is there—from one wanting to commune, only.

Pete Debree continues with no partners to head Inventions dot.com. Which remains highly profitable, on the market unruffled.

"And he can't see that his partner has died because something can't occur—yet something occurs, so that (action) isn't communing either."

It is for Grace. Grace and her officers and Captain Jasper Frank are subjected to grueling interrogation by high-ranking U.S. military interrogators. They are not tortured but they are not allowed lawyers present at these sessions nor are they allowed representation at all. Authority lost the sense that there *is* justice because it has pretended. Dirk cold, removed, interviews Grace. Pressing his steely eyes together he slaps her face. The blows cause the tears to stream down her face her eyes bruised shut.

In the hall, Officer Cloe O'Brien sees a boy dragged by his neck removed (after questioning) by two policemen. It's Esau de Light. She knows that the boys, slaves, taken in will be executed.

As promised, Monty on the side negotiates this precinct's police officer's lives. Their lives for the laptop's information (is the deal that's communicated to Grace only through Mr. Monty). Captain Frank doesn't agree. The police arrest and charge Pete Debree. Pete Debree's lawyers, coming before Judge Deli, can shift the focus to Debree's dead partners. The capital is tunneled in structure behind there a ghost. Emilia Hart, Debree's assistant, gives the frozen look as if that outside yet appearing as a structure indirectly sustaining her everything who thereby doesn't even need that without even mentioning herself yet one/any not having first praised her parents are not directly spoken to ever.

Pete Debree reminds Grace of an armadillo, the shy eyes touching one, when they've stepped close speaking to each other. But only that guise for an instant from him, lights killing.

She loves Pete Debree in a way. She's looking now at his files after Captain Jasper Frank goes ahead with the investigation anyway, refusing the deal. Grace bends for her eyes are so bruised shut she can barely see. She has nothing to do with servitude there. Emilia Hart freezing in the air, as if nothing went before her and her parents, or had, brings files to the table nonetheless in that Pete Debree smiles gently to Emilia Hart only, tolerant of Grace merely, without commenting on her blue bulbs. Yet Grace is unconcerned. Is solitary now. Working on the file beside her, Andrew trembles with anger.

Talk for Panel on 'My/One's Own Relation to Acker': Kathy Acker—Subjectivity, Plagiarism as Autobiography: Disruptive Practice

Acker proposes that her text *is* the other text.

The connection between reading and community is continually formed by writing that's disrupting real-time events.

"Influence" is past-tense, hierarchical. But this is as space.

My sense of Acker's view of present time[1]: being held to the absolute present (change) is pain—time as it is change is pain. Because "I'm scared."

Acker's project is always her autobiography as completely separated from its subject. All parts in her narratives, regardless of which character is speaking are in the same speaking voice: identical, seems to come from the same person. Thus 'character' is random, nonintentional plot—yet irretrievably formed—by violence ("art is elaborating violence"[2]). This 'is' the author but only as if mechanistically recreating her autobiography continually, as if speaking to someone else while making up random events-the-future only as 'spoken' off-the-cuff. The impression is that 'written' (as if it were 'speaking' only) doesn't exist *there* (in hers, though the narrative exists only as text). The text is thus secret as revelation of a life that is made-up (though the events are real/her life or real in the sense of being [in], rather than referring to these, events from other texts).

That is, 'character' and action for Acker is only imitation-of-oneself-as-if-she-is-speaking-unpracticed-monologue (an action), not *in* conversation (conversation is secret). The actions (events of the narrative) are connectives, go on as if spurts of whim which cause each other, cause new details thus *not* connected as crafted pre-formed ('written') plot. There are only new connectives arising. The dots in the paragraph of which the above sentence is part indicate that an original exists from which she supposedly quotes, part of which is apparently omitted; proposes her writing is 'only' appropriation (of other texts, of herself, of historical events), the text not distinguishable from 'its' original.

Referring to Cézanne and the Cubists, Acker makes her space in *Great Expectations* the same as theirs: "They found the means of making the forms of all objects similar. If everything was rendered

---

1. *Don Quixote*, Kathy Acker, Grove Press, New York, 1989, pages 51-52

2. *Great Expectations*, Kathy Acker, Grove Press, New York, 1989, p. 123

in the same terms, it became possible to paint the interactions between them. These interactions became so much more interesting than that which was being portrayed that the concepts of portraiture and therefore of reality were undermined or transferred."[3] "A narrative is an emotional moving."[4] Something exists at all when it is part of a narrative.

This is what I call (in my writing) minute movements within even tiny events which *are* the reality that's being undermined that's 'baseless' because they're only interactions (not entities). Acker was a Buddhist.

While in her oeuvre the most constant *reference* to action is to fucking or being fucked, fucking is evoked/takes place as social-political rather than physiological sensation (secret). Even that which is physiological is caused by the outside, done to one/though one acts in the outside/one does not 'express' (be in or write) direct sensation: "After the jeeps and the lorries left, wounded on the forehead now by the rising sun, I placed my sackcloth jacket over my face."[5]

Sensation is outside as a means of making the compressed space of psychological, physiological and landscape the same. A passage beginning "Now we're fucking": is entirely speaking: what she wants, speaking of herself as an image of a blonde tiger all over him, speaking what's happening and isn't happening, as if radio sex. A disembodied voice is sensation. The reader, as writer also, is not able to see or feel because the text has substituted for feeling. The text/speaking is between it. Text has to *be* the conditions only.

Acker's subject is subsumed in her (own) social construction in a benign, even beautiful universe. She constructs the site/sight/space (characters) of herself being enslaved because this *is*

---

3. *Empire of the Senseless*, Kathy Acker, Grove Press, New York, 1988, p. 25

4. *Great Expectations*, Kathy Acker, Grove Press, New York, 1989, p. 81

5. *Ibid.*, p. 58

occurring outside in the *social* realm everywhere, is realistic. The surface of the writing-as-the-enslavement is not palatable (the enslavement-as-the-writing is intended *not* to be palatable), one can not bear to be in it (the writing destroys itself, can't be dwelled in, changes the reader).

It is free by its nonintentional mode.

Plagiarism is: not allusion. It is 'the same.' The author as plagiarist: complete transformation as one's own appearance is invasion, destruction—that's continual realignment of oneself as same one. Autobiography as fiction: the same one is consuming (as *being*) itself.

If the transformation of one is continual it is the destruction of that one in *only* its appearance again.

In that sloth is non-transformative, it is a relation to terror still without being changed by it.

'The Senseless'—and the Senses

In this version, Robespierre was not guillotined and later in life is a *conservative*. Yet adhering to the same views and actions as before that were to root out the self of others.

They're not to be given (allowed) attention or to practice attention (which implies a self who is in attention—seeing itself as in a transitory action).

The figure of Robespierre is puritan so stringent there is no father—and as one form of patriarchy: only there is no love, only tyranny.

The present: U.S. convention stemming from puritan: the elect are successful, if we're suffering this means we're not God's elect. A corollary is the elite fashion that 'reification of self' is an evil; it is applied to Other only (authority's hypocrisy): as Other is seeming to reify by seeing being at all—as if they (Other) should not want to apprehend, or as if there were not any causing of any thing. We're not to see what causes or to be flesh, sensation, action. The sense of puritans (God's elect) a *sense* by being unknown (empty, as culture) is for Robespierre singular power. In the same fashion one sees a moon orbiting outside? When?, physical and sight and conceptual (the same as each other). Puritans hate the outside. They are not realistic.

He can't/won't see the relation of reification of self and *causal*, which *is* reification of self. What is mind action (reification) of self (self being only mind action, in sensation, in theory...)?

The outside is empty as the inside in his language—has no relation to phenomena, action. Empty except for hatred. Only his. Because Other's feeling is self.

The language is empty, we don't know what we are. Not even logic.

Acker therefore had to empty the language. She separates him from his language. The senseless.

We're animals who miraculously can hate. Acker's run-on sentences (with phrases separated by commas) are not many actions of others held together in one Wolfian 'moment of being'; but rather are sensory input to (of) many at once—are the same as actions outside—are not controlled by one. "I want: every part changes (the meaning of) every other part so there's no absolute/heroic/dictatorial/S & M meaning/part the soldier's onyx-dusted fingers touch her face orgasm makes him shoot saliva over the baby's buttery skull..."[6]

I have to make physical, sight, and conceptual the same as 'reification (motions) of self' in order to see phenomena. I am the time being. There is no influence, only present, hearing or reading.

Description of my text *The Tango*: "The text's internal debate is the author's comparison of *her* mind phenomena to exterior phenomena, laying these alongside each other actually—such as the mind's comparison to dawn, to magnolias, to color of night, as if these are manifestations of mind phenomena, which they are *here*. Placing one's mind-actions beside magnolias (words). The same figure repeated everywhere, a

---

6. *Empire of the Senseless*, Kathy Acker, Grove Press, New York, 1988, p. 26

line or passage may recur exactly as slipping out of, returning to, slipping out of, a frame of concentration and sound."[7]

Differentiate Acker. Acker empties the language by plagiarizing one self (source) and substituting in that same place or spot (at that self) another self (another source) which she's plagiarizing. In *Great Expectations*, she's plagiarizing Dickens, but in the pages of it's being Dickens it's de Sade and Proust, Keats, Japanese poetic diaries, and *The Story of O* at once but only *as* (as if it *is*, and by *displacing*) Acker.[8] Her same speaking and her 'life' (only her events).

My sense is his tyranny is to have only doctrine, rather than, and therefore obliterating, the motions of phenomena. (Acker says "interactions.") He replaces outside. Whereas motions-as-only-there are phenomena, doctrine is merely description. Whereas, Acker rejects having any theory-base that is not it's disruptive practice. See a person's mind phenomena as a shadow, only motion of apparent objects and events, cast on that person's language, backlit. Acker does that via plots?

Acker's self can only be there *then* (as Proust and de Sade's literary events there). By *only* reifying theirselves at once. That are empty by being their plots as interactions with (in) her real time and space. They're just repeated plots, so the self/same-as-text is outside actions even. Even actions are past-tense only—there is no present. That is the struggle, to be the present as all of it.

Robespierre can't dictate us. We take the place of theory-tyranny by substituting the (one's) motions of struggle. Taking the place of it with aping, there's only illusion-that-text-is-self.

In the fall, multiple explosions occur (at dawn New York time, and simultaneously on the west coast) demolishing sites of corporations, all on 'Andrew's list.' Security guards warned to leave by anonymous phone calls, there were no deaths from the

---

7. *The Tango*, Leslie Scalapino, Granary Books, New York, 2001

8. *Great Expectations*, Kathy Acker, Grove Press, New York, 1989, p. 8

explosions. The computer systems of these corporations and of Inventions dot.com and TORRID dot.com were hacked, their systems destroyed. Simultaneously, a number of assassinations of the U.S. military were carried out, two at their homes where they were living in Bogotá. The day after these events, a man walks up to Grace Abe on the street and hands her an envelope, then disappears into the walking crowd. Inside is a letter:

> Dear Grace,
> The Colombian people are held in the grip of the drug-growers, the guerrillas, and the government. These oppose but also collaborate with each other and with the U.S. military which foments war and encroaches as a power in Colombia. The U.S. is also trafficking in drugs.
> I was a scout. I am not human. A slave but developed with no cartridge in my head, feeling.
> emotion is produced present
> and sent in a poem. escaped, my job was to identify the money laundering operation (its participating corporations), the tie of U.S. business and military to Colombian drug trade. I was to contact members of FARC in the U.S. who deal with the U.S. military, and to persuade FARC to shortchange your military, to hold back in delivery while receiving weapons and money, representing this as being a deal with the Colombian government (which FARC is usually fighting): FARC would keep all profits. In reality, it was to cause a split between the U.S. military and FARC which would cause elimination of some and flush into the open people on the U.S. side. Your army removed Winter after torturing him (for what reason we don't know; probably Debree and Phil Wilson wanted him removed, their greed). Our operators, boys who were slaves, took out Wilson, a FARC chief.

(The owl. Wilson. The guys at Melinka's apartment were C.I.A. swarming thinks Grace. The people we killed in the rain.)

> I wanted to find my younger brother that only by there being no parents at all. He was still enslaved. Before my probable death here, I wanted to locate and free him. But he was killed before I could find him.
> I am writing this in the event of my death. I send my love to you. As I have been known to you—(there is no reason to know me otherwise), Your Antonio

Grace stunned, ponders this. did he mean her to turn over his letter to the Feds, thus identifying the recent insurgency?

might target the responsible or new slave group behind this in Colombia; he did not intend this? And if she turns over his letter revealing his personal relation to her, she will be under greater scrutiny and pressure than she is already. She burns the letter. His ghost but which only stands in the room for an instant.

Now she's mad. He has no beliefs. Robespierre, the director, has replaced her when she did the motions. In this version, Robespierre the glittering purity makes strawmen functions to grovel take the hit for him before him while he secretly which everyone sees is a mamma's boy with ladies lying to him whom he enlists/stings, one carried in a sedan chair, but he appears to glitter because no one can bear to feel/comprehend that they would, or could, allow themselves to be bullied only, therefore he must be of high ability they have to feel. This is a relief. It shows people feeling and similar. She stops crying.

At once Bush the outside, slack-mouthed so eyes squint as he yaps a jackal at killing, which he can't even envision apparently carried by bestial robots who strategize war everywhere that's unprovoked by recipients. The old frightened by death of everyone, there are no senses.

Text as Delicate slate forest the water-desert
(Pal Mal Comic)

Half of the ocean in sight/being (mid ocean in the Pacific) is delicate slate that is at the horizon. A horizontal slab of surface of mid-ocean is delicate slate.

Rough delicate slate forest the water-desert. Yet there it is divided in the middle half mid-ocean before us is heavy black moving. But we are on the surface (of the ocean).

(At 4:00 in the morning calling up outside in the city of people who homeless wake up, I thought in flashes I'd be homeless there if it were not for one thing now.)

Slate or onyx black plowing *on* the ocean surface (can't be beneath, except a submarine) is divided but without boundaries. In the Pacific it's middle rough delicate slate forest heavy the water-desert. _I_ lived on the ocean on freighters crossing it. There is nothing that is the sensory there. It doesn't exist, hasn't even.

Onyx charges of heavy midst of banks ocean not memory is its lines, for instance. On this surface.

The man first attacks and replaces me with a younger woman who is to only replace my words. (Nothing in her self, either.) Then, he says about Daniel Defoe that his character who's Moll Flanders committing illegal actions which are simply absorbed flattening as bringing onto one space, which is the space occurring _I_ make in a work called _Defoe_ in which the character, the Other, is Moll Flanders—the man saying Daniel Defoe did this space (where _I_ had written on surface of Daniel Defoe's writing as its/outside's actions [interior/exterior/ _'neither of these' being/is 'there' also_] absorbed on one space flattening space but it is what's unknown/not there) claims this as his own but as critical _idea_/exterior ('about' something else; so it is past and not an action), omitting a <u>one</u> and present time.

In this version, Robespierre is not guillotined and is later a fake. Robot theory become that, which is now 'any theory is lies.' Direct observation has become: removed by him. No One can keep up.

Alfredo Jaar refers in three columns of texts (on the wall)[1] to mines and to air sight. Nelson Mandela and his fellow inmates on Robbins Island in isolation for forty-one years, in summer 1964 were taken, chained together, and at a limestone quarry in the center of the island, put to work breaking rocks and digging lime. The lime was used to turn the island's roads white. At the end of the day, the black men had been turned white with lime dust. As they worked, the lime reflected the glare of the sun, blinding

---

1. Alfredo Jaar's installation, Lament of the Images, Galerie Lelong, New York, November, 2002.

the prisoners. Their repeated requests for sunglasses to protect their eyes were denied.

Another column of his texts refers to U.S. air strikes on Afghanistan, carpet bombing from B-52s flying at forty thousand feet, more than fifty cruise missiles President Bush said would avoid civilian causalities. Before launching the air strikes, the secret Defense Department bought an exclusive contract from IKONOS Space Imaging Inc., to all the air images of Afghanistan and neighboring countries. Although having satellite imaging of more than ten times the power, their possessions of the images produced a whiteout preventing western media from seeing the effects of the bombing. No one *here* can verify or refute Bush's claims. The CEO of Space Imaging Inc., said, "They are buying all the imagery that is available." There is nothing left to see.

After is—Alfredo Jaar's blinding light panel in room; and in a room, vault with slit of blinding light captured crack, which opens every six minutes as blinding light.

Here any life has the value of nothing as people accept, or look forward to—doing away with others, one people after another, being Armageddon.

Bush a single individual who is the outside now, can't see anything as real.

And neither can Robespierre, the inside-private, whose minute enmeshed delusions are finer and finer. For destruction of others only. Yet a mesh of X is not either on or in onyx waves of mid ocean, yet there.

One carried in a sedan chair (who apprehending the gestures of others, themselves erased because no one reads, has translated their gestures as ideas only, rather than there being their movements, which in her work she says are her ideas to have credit for these) (academizing motions).

While one by one, before them, he erases *other* women. (and others) But then, she has to consider that they (carried), not the others erased, *want* this, while being duped at once.

There are birds before or forest—oneself is the view.
Who only sees outside before one. The birds have no space
that's the birds-trees behind them. no Delicate slate forest—delicate space forest is in front of them, only one.

24. ANDREW

For the woman in *Terminator 2*, change of interior-subjective occurs 'outside.' 'One's to change everything at every moment in structure' therefore.

They are ripping off the people's resources and defining these people to themselves marginalized in their own land as "undeveloped" while the invasion of same-image-making pod-flowers is occurring from a separate source. Separate from either of these, figures zap—with stapler-like cattle prongs in crowds that infuse digitalis—hearts, killing seemingly randomly. One's heart hurts. As if in tall waving grass on all sides in streets, crossing, the hearts in the crowd are hit by the prongs and people down trembling with the grass waving around them some dying tremble.

Clinging to the bag in the high atmosphere, breathe that way. In sleep. Carry the long bag beside one at day, so that the involutes, folds of the outside are in one. The lids of his friend, the bulging seams closed, exude poisonous liquid (on the seams of his friend's closed eyes), embittered in its surface because it's a demon. Pear trees, it's the Middle Ages here. The lids closed trash the poisonous person as an angry being they mirror, the same one. They think the tears aren't theirs. (When they had tears on their face. Singular.) To 'feel' 'for' someone. As if these feelings are absolved by being 'taken' or 'felt' by someone else— *interiorly* the actions 'do' *not* occur in *them*, if one 'feels' *'for'* them.

How does one end feeling pain with pain? Andrew's nature being serene is not passive. Not always angry sitting out at a café.

To the side, in the air, is only the visual event of the military appearing alike bobbing in exposed open trucks, continual events, on the roads everywhere on the desert high mountains, the sparse populace persecuted, yet adhering to practice of attention to their conceptual projections, as illusional, even having the military who torture as the reflections by which these very constructions can be seen. Seeing then make a leap because of that that entirely clarifies them. But they may be eliminated. Their social-seeing—entirely, their civilization—crowd eliminated. The packed trucks of military overseeing who persecute, who see 'commercially as if that were life, and were pleasure in life,' yet the high thin altitude mountain crags rest on thin day-moon continuously? Only apparently, moon on one day. One in traveling there.

This ability may be eliminated by tyranny in the structure.

Grace sitting out at a café. For her at least that which is in the visual plain is free, isolated. A dun-brown pad of face has emerged from the high waving grass, seated.

At one of the tables a man with dun-brown moist soft pad of nose, as if taking up the entire of the face yet not distinct making the eyes muted, was there. He'd emerged from the high grass.

She gets up with her purse and leaves to follow him.

In the visual plain, her partner with her, no longer fellow officer, as they've quit, lazily sipping his cappuccino watches her go, an indigo hot evening beginning—where there had been the evening before, no day even with it.

A line of trucks is going by, which the dun-pad-nose is joining. They stop, expelling exhaust, so that he might mount them. Immediately, Grace and Andrew run to the trucks, Cloe appearing on the roof of a building across the street training a gun on them. The cargo of the trucks are boys being carried to execution. The partners release them into the evening. One of these is Esau de Light who floats off the truck.

Her partner's mind, completely separate from the indigo evening, any, duplicates seeing hacking and crushing a pod that had been resembling, thus killing, a citizen who was slumped in a door sleeping. He'd done this hacking. The citizen not dressed in a military suit. Yet here and there military suits emerging on the liquid-worms are all around him, so that he runs on.

At other times, he responds to Grace seeing her applying the drug on the burn marks on her naked chest which 'causes' a later clear elation running hunting. She's addicted to "struggle," but may have lost ability to do it, as that which is exterior, to apprehend is interiorized. Then he said gently as she applied it to the burn marks Don't Grace. Though one time he pauses, softly cracking a joke, You've been given grace.

Holding the bag curled beside it at night, breathing from it, the accordion only moving softly (she makes it do it) clings to the bag. One's organs and veins come apart in the high atmosphere. Only the bag is suffusing breathing, which is outside, so one has no movement of one's outside. *The dream of the spine.* The subjective interior *is* alleviated—of one—in life by change outside. Therefore we're not bound to continual rebellion. Only in one's present? O, not at all in one's present?

To *write* only exterior 'actions' that are in events (that are in 'the outside only') in order to change 'interior-subjective' ones— as if 'interior' is vast geographical tracks—is to separate from either 'outside' or any 'interior.'

The relation of memory to event *is* separation. They aren't the same. Actions are not lost roaming, in that they are not a memory (of their occurrence). The dream of the spine.

The actual chrysalis liquifies and 'then' is the other thing, butterfly. But there has to be 'work' or 'instructions' 'to' liquify and then reform it—the 'written' 'instruction' isn't either the chrysalis or the butterfly yet. Is the written instruction indelible? DNA. *Secret Autobiography,* however, is neither instructions nor fiction—all events are fictions (events at all are only their sequence).

Some people were kept as slaves in the colony, an urban embroiled Mars. If they want to consume them they do. They extract further concessions, then call public lists to make further examples. Groups of five were tied together, beaten, hundreds marching on roads, some dying still tied to the others. *One day waking recently she had no memory of any of the incidents of life at all later or before.* Because of the physical pain. "Representatives" of their original people are in official bureaus, look disdainfully but without speaking when they meet in public. But one has no memory at all suddenly. Blossoms opened on the trees before dark roses are everywhere. In the day there's a bright moon *only*. Without relation with people in space.

Officer Cloe O'Brien, a long slender leg draped while she's seated by the half-groups like half-life so their interior is visible in cafés. People in clusters on the street illumined from the golden ground, bending at some who are consumed as liquid worms there then running on as these move. Cloe finds Grace who is with only an innocent expression kneeling on one of the figures (these figures simply kill people on the street).

'The media,' 'the news' (business only is "freedom" as if "information"), 'presents' of events as if they were actually exterior, as if that which is business is the order in which events occurred.

Tibetan *Secret Autobiography* 'is to see' what is particular and recognized, *as illusions,* thus shared later by the community. But these visions only occur (later accepted, identified) as secret, in the sense of not being spoken (not being shared, and thus 'formed'), before being written. *(I also see my simple illusion by—not perceiving it before writing. By not doing so. Spoken it would have been something else, I wouldn't see it.)*

Being the silken worm that *is* itself pod-flower transforming as oneself, sometimes one is consumed. (In the film, one *is only* consumed and perception is irrelevant except as a warning that one should flee.)

'Interiority' seized by the outside, translates it only. 'Interiority' which admits the outside but does not move—as if the outside floats separate in its midst—neither eschewing the outside nor incubating it. Not creating it. Is *Secret Autobiography* 'interiority not moving the outside floating in it yet not reflected in it (and the outside not reflecting one's interiority)'—so that neither produces or eschews the other—as different instants of this occurring?

Secret Autobiography: written therefore secret experience by 'seeing,' that's *not* exteriorized in life or in dreams as events (which are exteriorizations *only*).

There was a line between the writing being simply narrative of an event and being its impermanence. That an event 'referenced' might be so minute that later the event can't even be remembered is part of the writing's (being the event's) *occurrence as impermanence.*

SECRET AUTOBIOGRAPHY

There was an endless field of emerald green, tiny clover clusters, and area further on of deep purple 'clover,' no blossoms, rather was dark purple tiny soft clusters. On it there were huge dark weasel-shaped animals attacking horses. They were running in circles. The horses and the dark weasel-shapes attacking them. I entered the purple clover on my bare left side thigh saying to T that there were millions of bumblebees which I then saw, and was not dipping my feet into the vast field.

I was in a room of men who were plump dressed in white though they were soldiers and were about to leave for a combat. A plump man in white asking me to provide him with (a particular) white cat which, when I have, was in a metal cage with the man who was stretched kneeling interceding with it. So I thought I shouldn't have put them together though it had seemed to be his. The cat was extended up like a white fan fur up humped spokes out, enraged, with him kneeling out to it.

'*as* one's mind is,' but that isn't exterior events
a falcon killed a bird by my head at night. when I lay night surrounded by a garden. *night night*
this was the event *as* my mind. also. the falcon killing the bird was outside in night. beside my ear. the event occurred and as memory is 'random' now.

first outside roses so red they were awe filled sails walking
the flowers weren't before one or after one walking

a cut into the back out slowly the people here and there
before roses so red they're not communicative to bees for them
they're unto themselves while the people don't want to speak,
to the one, from convention

but there are only birds out any place. low. everywhere

He's out flat on the unobstructed sand so there's a silver
round moon faint at the edge, a disc in the sky at the same time
as the sun. on the other side. It's at the rim, who's flat a former
hood.
The silver moon hangs over what are pink mounds, from
the other. So that at that moment he's flat where there's no one
to see him. as having a reality in this. that is eliminated, and from
him.

The bud's flattened on its own. Cattle come along side.
They're standing in the sky on a small ledge but it's dusk. The
disc is hanging behind them making them dark and flat from the
front. The newspaper says a man in the sea was floated by a
tortoise. This is the difference between event and what it says.
The bud opens, seeing them, though it can't see.

The dream I had is closer to being because it abuts it—then.
before it's occurred. This is in the present. The blossoms on the
plum trees opened. On some. Birds sit, and fly amongst branches
of bare trees. It has no reverse side, and is thin.
Birds skim low by me.

So the flapping swans here so they're the same as the sky simply flying is that (in time), before.

The entire day completely dilated is flapping in one's recesses so it is behind in the back of one. Stagnant in that sense, as it's flapping and then narrowing it in front though it's still the day.

It's the day in a sense, narrowed to a thin disc in front in which the entire dilated day behind in the recesses of oneself bangs shuttering on it. The day collapses in that sense when that's slowed and interminable.

Event in which meeting LH and, before but at the same time of the occurrence, having the thought that "all of life is void" which I knew she'd want to hear rushing up to her, she was smiling, nothing said.

There were three parts to the event, the future in it known so that it was occurring at the same time first. Spitting in a donkey's eye was in the third part so it was as if it *has* occurred—early-on before it *has*. There's an incredible freedom, not having to worry.

Yet not action *there*, by being there. Spitting in the donkey's eye wasn't an action then (or *there*). It occurred then (earlier in it) but not by being an *action*.

There was a wide plaza surrounded by monumental buildings as in the capital, and across the huge empty space I herded two identical gray horses attached at the sides by a black pole. A few people were far away in the plaza.

Then I was in a garden. Someone held up the plants on stems to show that the stalks, floating upright on top of the earth's surface, were not growing on it. Were existing with no roots. A wildcat right there (which was yellow-spotted with dark dipped fox's tail) had done this.

The wildcat had removed the basis (of the stems). So I moved to cut the wildcat off from leaving. To stop it (as to chide its behavior). It indicating springing on me, a pre-dream virtual reality vision occurred of it leaping and tearing me up without this action being done in fact. 'That that would occur.' So that I moved aside then not barring its path. ('then' see 'the wild cat was myself.')

I was crawling to swans on huge emerald embedded sets of fields—crawled 'with' my neck disk pressing on the spinal cord in fiery inexpressible pain. Pursued them to look at them. In fact. And not a pair (that the event occurred—or that is initiating action)

"white green"—'no'—occur in one in dream in a forest

walking—there not being any—separation between 'that'—being in forest—there

only—but the dream is "whitish" rim, 'no eyes'—there—isn't in one

—is in the dream.—pair only—are 'that.'—"white green" night—is.

the two huge realms—not in one—occur

Dream PW (so recent past is 'to try to' 'wreck one's mind' [by] placing states together which can't exist at the same time) is to be transported out (of danger) by the resistance ('behind the lines'), guerrilla fighters—I've dropped him off (I'm remaining behind) and he's waiting on a bench, the pickup truck (AG driving, whom I don't know very well but who doesn't think) there (by high embanked dirt curbs). Packed with a small bundle. I look to see if he gets in the pickup, which he will.

Later waking, the important thing is I have no sense of *my* leaving (though he is). Waking see the dirt streets are Rangoon, where I was as

        a kid for a short time—so that it won't exist again (or continue).

Waking, the dream is two events at the same time— being in Rangoon almost a child, with only a sibling, in utter freedom

        which hadn't been in my mind in the dream

To be the outside—in real-time I'm exhausted in that everything outside is to be translated *thought as convention*—I was trying to translate 'there not being an instant between two instances' as a thought so as to be that action only. But trying is stringing me out.

        so the dream is—to translate at the same time.—and is the two at once

        the dream is, almost child (no longer existing) in utter freedom *then*

        is unknown in the dream, yet *is it*, and is the same time as *to translate as it*—only which is a thought but *not* constructing that social existing that's here (here, the outside, is what thought *is*)

        the dream's utter freedom

        Walking in Mongolia in fact on vast gold ground as if it illumines the dark indigo sky, its day-cobalt. So it wasn't night or day time that separates, or the huge gold plain on which I was walking—it didn't separate from dark dark blue that's illuminated from it (the plain). There were no trees. Invisible birds sang.

Blooming night is not dream, isn't yet there of having to go through a 'check place' as if soviet, and other couriers aren't that either, to then deliver for them something which one doesn't know, lose the instructions while there foresee outside doors of 'check place' along dark bank of poplars.

[no, that was just a dream; it was not seeing.]

Yet one figure sits on the huge lit green floor, stripped to the waist with his arms raised. The immense luminous billowed cloud sky is passing over him. Or Atlantis, the green floor flat lit is passing by its roof. Horses run on the floor.

Only horses live in this land, the flat green floor surrounded by the lit domes of hills which are as if underneath it. As if the mountains and flat floor were submerged under water when that isn't occurring, isn't visible. A colt is so young, it's lying resting on its side whereas they stand. They walk together. Yet one man is there lying on his side raised on his elbow on the green floor.

is subjunctive—the man starving dying lying in garbage?—there not being black dawn—?
no. not anyway—that is, anywhere.—or: subjunctive is *only* 'social.' both.

then (when alive).—(subjunctive.)—black dawn isn't?—so it has to pass. both.

bound as 'split' (one's) 'to' conception of change as, or in, behavior—
that was not when a child

rather than in blossoming trees—everywhere as
ground is an ocean here

so 'split' is *that* only—ocean 'in' blossoming trees—
'in fact' has to be to change people's behavior/one's as
sole

—one's subjectivity/language is their or one's *motion*
only there?

seeing being only a motion even (in walking, say)

one has no back—yet.—not even 'in' 'night'—not
even past movements' 'night'—either—and is
future 'nights'
where(?) no movement of one's occurs—future is
same as one's motions without extension *now*

one's motion ahead—is only one *now*—nights rose

wall standing rose could just
'place'
together
as evening in the middle of
people
speaking
and so no space even there
one?

Always stay in
the quiet illumined grass
land—but I can't—do it
there being other people there

to
just do
it only staying in the grass land
illumined
'place' it together is 'land' and
comes out
just
do it
examin
ing
dreamed looking down
in
bush that's huge forest leaveless
fan
my needing place to live in dream, the
next day
see forest leaveless fans hill up
vertically
light leaveless array fan
is this the same as

—is leaves, both—seeing.—

examin
ing
the forest rose wall as
white in outside
and
dark green early forest not different
from rose
after (it) rose leaveless fan-
dawn
one?

cold—freezing red sky dusk—slice, reduction not existing—
walking only as clear—one—outside, dark roses are in it, as
freezing
    red's slice

    a half of the night seen, which isn't there yet—sky only is
there—at all

    bright dark roses—not bud, ever—in the slice only